# TWO GUNS WEST

When Bodie and Brand arrive in San Francisco, searching for a kidnapped young woman, the city by the bay doesn't exactly welcome them with open arms. But danger has never stopped these two before — not even when it comes in the form of a deadly Chinese Tong determined to extend its opium empire as far as the east coast. With the help of Captain Richard Hunt, a British agent from Jamaica, all they have to do is bring the Tong — and its murderous criminal contact Milo Traeger — down . . .

D0610620

NEIL HUNTER

# TWO GUNS WEST

*Complete and Unabridged*

**LINFORD**
*Leicester*

First published in Great Britain in 2016

First Linford Edition
published 2018

A catalogue record for this book is available
from the British Library.

ISBN 978–1–4448–3945–6

Published by
F. A. Thorpe (Publishing)
Anstey, Leicestershire

Set by Words & Graphics Ltd.
Anstey, Leicestershire
Printed and bound in Great Britain by
T. J. International Ltd., Padstow, Cornwall

This book is printed on acid-free paper

# Prologue

Milo Traeger had never been a man to waste his life on labor, hard or otherwise. He preferred to make his money by other means. If it meant out-and-out thievery, he would choose that way, though elaborate schemes were also what he excelled at. Fraud, swindling, anything that would increase his wealth was fair game.

And Traeger loved the game. He had started his life of crime in his early twenties so that now, in his late thirties, he was fully committed to his nefarious ways. It involved conning people out of large amounts of money. Traeger had little in the way of morals or conscience. Twice he had committed murder when a plan went awry. The latest, no more than six months ago, had been an elderly woman he had cheated out of over fifty thousand dollars. When she had confronted him and accused him of the crime of larceny, Traeger had realized he needed to silence her before she went public. For Traeger, it was an act of self-preservation. He had entered the old woman's home at night, choked her, and had vanished.

But his desperate act had been his undoing. The old lady had confided in her nephew, telling him of her suspicions. Her sudden death had kindled a need for the banker to find out the truth and had started an unofficial investigation into Traeger's background. When witnesses came forward, a case was generated that revealed Traeger had been involved in other schemes to defraud. On this occasion, he had taken a step too far, and promptly vanished. The banker, who had a large circle of diversely influential acquaintances, brought his plight to bear on those friends; and one of those friends, in the law enforcement world, had a quiet word with someone in the Justice Department.

That man was Frank McCord.

With the facts in front of him, presented by the banker's investigation, McCord, realizing he was being pressured by people above and beyond his department, accepted the unspoken request to look into the matter. McCord was no politician, but he saw the writing on the wall. Turning down the assignment could have rebounded on him at a later date. Doing the bidding of those higher up the ladder would do him no harm when it came to maintaining his department. So he took it on board; and as Jason Brand was not involved in any assignments at the time, the contents of the file were waiting for him when he returned to Washington following his break visiting with Virginia Maitland and his son, Adam.

As usual, McCord wasted little time getting down to the business at hand, detailing the background of the case and how figures from above were pushing for the case to be investigated by Justice. 'Before you say anything,' McCord said, 'this is me under protest.

So it's no good looking at me like that. Let's do it. Get it off the books and keep a smile on our faces.'

Brand read the reports. The added files from McCord's own investigation. The man had his own informers, some of whom lived on the fringes of the criminal world and provided useful information from time to time, keeping McCord apprised of interesting facts. Brand found a number of those facts very interesting. By the end of the study, he already had enough information to make his first move.

The file mentioned Traeger's dealings. Thieving from his victims and suspicion of murder. His current foray into an association with the San Francisco Tong and Kwai Fu Tong — and opium.

★　★　★

By this time, Traeger was embarking on what he saw as the biggest scheme of his life. If it succeeded, he would have it

4

made, with no more need to work mundane tricks. There was a down side, but he passed that off as an acceptable risk. The people he was hoping to ally himself with were not the kind who tolerated any wrongdoing within their world. Traeger figured it was worth the risk, because if it paid off he would have everything he wanted.

His new partner-to-be was a high-up member of a Chinese Tong, based in San Francisco and under the hand of Kwai Fu Tung, the Tong Master. The ultimate authority. A man who wielded great power and was known to have little patience with anyone who wronged him or his organization.

Traeger, always looking out for the next deal, had seen the potential in the sale and distribution of opium. He understood its addictive nature and saw there was unlimited scope to increase its sales. It would be a new venture for him, but one that could lift him to greater criminal heights.

At a bar he frequented, Traeger often

met one of his numerous contacts, a wiry, sharp-faced man called Duryea. From Duryea he had picked up snippets of information that when pieced together told Traeger he had the chance to move into a wider circle of the criminal world. He spent time seeking more details. Listening to talk and building his background until he was able to offer his services to Kwai Fu Tung by way of a carefully worded telegram to one of Tung's eastern operators.

He met the man in Chicago — neutral ground for both of them. Over a meal in the restaurant, Traeger outlined his plan to his contact, a florid-faced overweight man called Jellico who wore a loud checked suit and a flounced shirt.

'Your Mr. Tung wants to open a way he can distribute his opium in New York in larger quantities?'

'It's been on his mind for some time.'

'I believe I can help him do that.'

Jellico helped himself to thick slices of beef from the platter on the table. He had already cleared his plate and was ready for a second serving. Traeger watched as the man heaped more food on his plate.

'Tell me what you have in mind,' Jellico said.

Traeger drew his gaze from the sight of Jellico pushing food into his mouth. 'I've been doing some research. The way you people have been transporting opium is slow and only delivers small amounts.'

'That's because we have to be careful.'

'You need a legitimate cover that'll let you send larger amounts, delivered to New York and stored in a secure place waiting to be moved into the city.'

'All well and good — but can you offer that?'

'Yes. By the simple expedient of pushing it through an established company where it'll be stored in warehouses deemed honest and above board.'

'If the business is honest, how will you manage to do this?'

'By presenting the owner with a good

reason why he should play along.'

Jellico paused, his fork held in mid-air. 'Such as?'

'The man I have in mind has a daughter. His wife is dead and he dotes on the woman. If she was to be taken away, I'm sure he could be persuaded to do what we wanted.'

A slow smile curled Jellico's lips, moist from the juice of the beef he was devouring. The sight almost turned Traeger's stomach. 'You could make this happen?' Jellico said.

'Yes.'

'Out of the goodness of your heart?'

'No. By a working arrangement with Mr. Tung. A business arrangement that'll benefit both sides.'

Jellico finished his food and pushed his plate aside. He beckoned a waiter and ordered a pot of coffee to be brought to them in the quiet lounge next to the dining room. When they were settled with large cigars, Jellico asked Traeger to detail his proposal. By the time he had heard everything, Jellico was smiling broadly and eager to send a telegram to his employer.

★ ★ ★

A few weeks later, Traeger had his deal. The moment he had Tung's acceptance, he put his plan into operation.

While he'd been waiting for this, he'd worked on his contact, using financial incentives to find out what he needed. It was easy. Clyde Leeson was in debt to a local money lender. He had been borrowing cash to feed his gambling habit, which only got him in deeper because he was a reckless player. He never understood the meaning of not throwing good money after bad. The more he lost, the more he continued to play, with the forlorn hope his luck had to change. Unfortunately it didn't, and Leeson simply let his debts mount up.

Duryea had picked up on Leeson's misfortune and passed the information to Traeger. Duryea knew the loser worked for a wealthy man, and from what Traeger had been feeding him, realized Leeson might just be the man Traeger was looking for. Once Traeger had the lowdown, he knew he had found his man. He paid Duryea his finder's fee and moved in on his mark. After a few nights carefully watching Leeson dig himself in deeper, Traeger knew he had chosen well.

If the idea panned out, both Tung and Traeger's organization would benefit. Tung would deliver the opium, and Traeger's east coast people would distribute it. Everyone would profit from the deal. Just the thought pleased Traeger.

And as easy as that, it began . . .

# 1

Laramie, Wyoming

The day was calm, the sun warm. Bodie felt at peace with the world for the moment, though there was a restlessness growing in him to move on. Not from Ruby Kehoe, who was proving to be the best female company he had ever known. Yet he needed action; something other than what Ruby offered. Something to feed his brain and allow him to exercise his skills. The soft living in Laramie was getting to him. He was wearing new clothing, and Ruby had persuaded him to have his shaggy hair cut and groomed. It pleased her and that pleased him. Yet he still needed something to occupy him.

He was on his way back to the hotel, wondering where she was, when he saw her hurrying down the street to meet him, an expectant look on her face. Long gone were the dirty range clothes she had worn before. Now she had on a dress and all the feminine accessories to go with it. Her face was still beautiful and her hair flowed behind her, shiny and neat.

'Bodie,' she called, unmindful that young ladies were not expected to call out in the street. She was waving her hand at him, clutching a buff telegram paper. The last time she had brought one of those, it had been to confirm that her father's lawyer had negotiated with the authorities and Bodie's claim for the reward for the Gallman gang had been approved. Lawyer Bainbridge lived up to Ruby's promise, and he was able to pick up his money from a bank in town.

'I'd ease off there,' Bodie said. 'You'll bust right out of that damned dress if you're not careful.'

Her smile was almost dazzling. 'What — right here on the street? Mr. Bodie, what are you suggesting?'

He didn't pursue that line of thought. 'I take it you have something to tell me?'

She nodded, her face shining with excitement. 'It's a message from Lawyer Bainbridge. He has an offer for you. Not exactly a bounty hunt. He asks if you'd look for someone who's gone missing. The young daughter of a trusted friend in New York. An extremely important and wealthy man named Chin Yi Soong.'

'Hold on there. Try speaking slowly, Ruby. Remember I'm just a simple feller from the west.'

Her laughter seemed to fill the street, attracting curious glances. 'That's the last thing you are, Bodie. Now are you going to listen to me?'

'Yes, ma'am.'

'There will be money on offer, Bodie. I made certain that would be part of the offer. But it's important. Jasmine Yi Soong is a friend of mine as well. A beautiful young woman. She'd gone to visit relatives on the west coast, and had

13

been there for almost two weeks when she simply vanished. No one can find her. It appears she was taken off the street. I believe she's been kidnapped. Jasmine isn't a foolish young woman. She wouldn't do anything risky, or fail to keep in touch — unless she couldn't.'

'Has there been a letter demanding money? Anything like that?'

'Nothing. Not as yet. Her father is distraught, Bodie. His daughter's disappeared on the other side of the country, and he doesn't know what to do . . . '

Bodie took her arm and led her back up the street to the telegraph office. 'Send a message to the lawyer. Ask for everything known about your friend. Description. Any identifying marks. Whatever her father has. Send it now. Then we go and sit down at the hotel, and you tell me all about this Jasmine. And I mean everything.'

When they stepped out of the telegraph office, Ruby clung to his arm. 'Thank you,' she said.

'Once we have the information, I

need you to head back to New York. You stay close to the father. I'll contact you through Bainbridge. No games this time, Ruby. I don't expect to turn around and find you behind me in . . . hell, you said the west coast. But where?'

'Oh, I thought I'd said . . . it's San Francisco . . . '

★   ★   ★

Jasmine Soong

It had happened so fast that Jasmine had no chance to defend herself even if she had been able. In truth, there was little she could have done. She was a twenty-three-year-old woman with no idea what was happening. One moment she was walking alongside her female escort, enjoying the pleasant day, until two men rushed at her, attacked and struck down her escort and the male guide who followed behind, then bundled her into a covered buggy. She struggled, but they were too strong for her. In her immediate panic, she had tried to call out. A rough hand covered her mouth, pressing hard, and almost smothered her. Other hands yanked her arms behind her, and a coarse rope was bound around her wrists. When the hand was removed from her mouth, a thick gag replaced it. She was pressed back in the seat as the buggy rattled its way along the street, making frequent turns, swaying back and forth.

There was a man on either side of her, their bodies pressing against her. A third man was seated ahead, driving the buggy. No one spoke. With the side canopies pulled down, she was unable to see where they were going.

Jasmine was an intelligent young woman, and it quickly occurred to her — and she hoped she was correct — that she was in no immediate physical danger. Whoever these men were, they had kidnapped her with the intention of demanding something. Most likely from her father, who was an extremely wealthy man. She could not imagine there being any other reason. She admitted to a degree of naivety where the world was concerned. Her mind was unable to conceive of any other reason for her being taken. Unless it was for some kind of depravity . . . which she refused to consider, because she understood little of the coarser side of life.

She forced herself to remain calm. She was frightened and would have admitted it without hesitation. Her father had instilled in her not to allow fear to dictate her actions. He would have told her to wait until she knew what was happening before she abandoned hope. While she was still breathing, there was always hope. So she remained still and attempted to clear her mind of negative thoughts. It wasn't easy, but concentrating on it distracted her for the time being.

After what seemed a long time, the buggy came to a jerking stop. She had noticed that the sound coming from the wheels had changed from hard ground to something like timber. And the air bore the familiar odor of the ocean.

The side covers were pulled open, and she blinked against the sudden intrusion of bright sunlight. Her captors pulled her from the buggy, and she stared around her. Across a wooden wharf was indeed the ocean. It stretched out into the distance. When she turned her head, she saw large wooden warehouses running the length of the wharf. Seagulls swooped and wheeled in the sky over the area, their raucous cries filling the air.

One of the men removed her gag. 'Yell all you want, missy,' he said. 'Ain't nobody close enough to hear you.'

Jasmine gazed at him, a faint forced smile on her face. 'I don't yell or raise my voice,' she said. 'I imagine that would be more in your line.'

The man laughed. 'They said you were a snobby baggage. Just 'cause your dear papa has money don't lift you higher above the rest of us.'

'If you wish to believe that, I won't

attempt to correct you.'

The second man reached out to finger the material of her dress. She jerked away from him.

'I'd wager this dress cost more than anything we're wearing, Dugan.'

'Yeah? Well I don't give a damn. Under it she's just a bare-assed woman.'

'Maybe we should take a look and find out.'

'Brave men,' Jasmine said. 'Especially when the woman is all tied up and unable to fight back.'

Dugan grinned at her, showing his uneven teeth. 'Well, hell, lady, that's the way I like 'em.'

'Please keep your thoughts to yourself, Dugan.' The voice from behind them was soft, yet it commanded attention — and respect. When Jasmine turned, she found herself looking at a tall, lean Chinese man. His black hair was brushed straight back from his face. He stood with his hands behind his back, gazing at her with quiet interest. His eyes moved from her to Dugan and his partner. He was standing just inside the half-open doors of the warehouse, and was dressed in traditional Chinese clothing: black tunic and trousers, with soft-soled black shoes on his feet. He was Kwai Fu Tung — a San Francisco Tong Master.

'Escort the young lady inside, Mr. Dugan. I have things to discuss with her. Business matters of importance.'

Jasmine, for some inexplicable reason, felt she had nothing to fear from this man — for the moment at least. 'I doubt there's anything to discuss between us,' she said.

Dugan nudged her and she walked inside the warehouse, following Tung. Behind her, the big doors closed with a solid thud. The interior was packed with crates, bales, and stacks of wooden casks, and had a hot, musty smell.

Tung paused, turned, smiling benignly. 'On the contrary, Miss Soong; there is definitely much to discuss ... in the main the negotiations that will determine when — or if — you are returned to your father.'

With that declaration, Jasmine was forced to revise her earlier thought — that she was safe in this man's hands. She realized he wanted something from her, though at that moment she had no idea what. She also realized she would soon find out. Whatever is was, there would be nothing pleasant about it. Jasmine didn't have to think too hard to understand the reasons would involve her father. He was wealthy. Had many important connections. Knew extremely influential people both here in San Francisco and New York.

And there was something in the way Tung looked at her — as if she was little more than a piece of merchandise. The smile on his face was a shadow to cover the thoughts in his mind. Jasmine decided those thoughts would be directed towards her. At that moment, she fervently wished she was back home in New York — and in that same moment she wondered if she would ever see it again . . .

# 2

## San Francisco — California

Bodie found he was not overly fond of the city. It was too busy. Too noisy. He had never seen so many people in one place at the same time. He stood on the sidewalk outside the hotel that Lawyer Bainbridge had booked for him and watched the constant flow of people. He counted at least a half dozen nationalities in as many seconds. The same with the speech he picked up. Bodie thought of the wide empty spaces of the western landscape. There a man could go for days and not see a soul. The streets of Tombstone or Laramie were practically deserted compared to the jostling crowds here.

Over the rooftops of the buildings opposite, he could see the masts of the tall ships anchored in the bay. Since his arrival the evening before, Bodie had not had a chance to look the city over. The long, seemingly endless rail trip had left him weary, and he had gone directly to the hotel, and gone to bed. When he woke he took a long soak — the room had its own bathroom, with water on tap — and admitted he felt better after that. A shave, then down to eat a cooked breakfast and drink a number of cups of rich coffee.

He checked the oak-cased clock on the dining room wall a half hour before his arranged meeting with Henry Lee. Lee had been retained to assist Bodie in his search for the missing woman. From the information provided, Lee was employed by Chin Yi Soong in the West Coast division of his business. One of many employees. The young man, Bodie had been informed, was smart and to be fully trusted. He figured he would make up his own mind on that score.

Bodie took a seat in one of the upholstered chairs spread around the lobby. He sat facing the door, studying the flow of guests. They all suggested money to him. The men were dressed in expensive suits and the women wore dresses he decided were in fashion, whatever that implied.

It reminded him of his own attire before he had left Laramie. Ruby had insisted he attend a tailor in the town. She took no prisoners, having him outfitted in a dark two-piece suit and a white shirt and string tie.

'After all,' she said, 'you can't stroll around San Francisco like an out-of-work trail hand.'

'Never had problems before.'

'You have never been to San Francisco and stayed in one of the most expensive hotels before. Now stop grumbling and let the nice man measure you up.'

When he was finally dressed in his new duds, standing in front of a full-length mirror, Bodie had to admit she had not been wrong. He caught a glimpse of her reflection, a pleased smile on her face, nodding her approval.

'Mr. Bodie, you look positively handsome. Now all we need is to do something about those boots,' she said.

'Hell, no. The boots stay. I can't wear anything else.'

A compromise was reached when the tailor suggested he take Bodie's boots and have them cleaned and polished. 'You won't recognize them when my man has finished with them.'

Bodie slipped his boots off and handed them over. 'No tricks,' he warned. 'Better be the same boots when they come back.'

They were but looking better than they had on the day he'd bought them. Cleaned, buffed and polished.

'You see?' Ruby said. 'Trust me, Bodie, I won't let you down. Now we need to go and arrange your tickets for San Francisco.'

'One question. Why hasn't Soong hired professional help?'

'Like Pinkerton detectives?'

'Yeah.'

'Some years back he did hire them to investigate a problem within his company. There had been thefts from the accounting department. Unfortunately the detectives made errors, and the thief got away. Soong took them to court and won his case, but it left him with a mistrust for private detectives.'

'Hell, Ruby, I'm not even a detective, private or otherwise.'

'If Lawyer Bainbridge vouches for you, which he has, and Mr. Soong does, then I believe we're all happy.'

'I'm beginning to believe Lawyer Bainbridge pulls a lot of strings.'

'Believe it, Bodie. He is a man of great influence. He said to tell you if you have any problems in San Francisco, to telegraph him and he'll help. Make sure you don't forget that.'

The next day Bodie boarded the train, after a pleasant goodbye to Ruby. 'I just know you'll find Jasmine,' she said.

'That's a lot of faith you're carrying,' he'd replied.

'You saved me and brought me down off that mountain. I trusted you then. I trust you now.'

She stayed on the platform until the

train was out sight, offering Bodie a final wave.

★ ★ ★

Bodie was in a private Pullman suite that had everything he needed for the long trip. In the leather valise, Ruby had made sure he had extra clothing and had reluctantly packed his rolled gun rig and the .45 Peacemaker. As the train picked up speed out of Laramie, Bodie sat down and stripped the pistol, then cleaned and oiled it before thumbing in fresh cartridges, leaving an empty chamber under the hammer.

A gentle tap on the paneled door drew his attention. It was the attendant asking if he wanted any refreshments. Bodie ordered fresh coffee.

'We serve lunch at midday, sir.'

'Can you get me a table?'

The attendant smiled. 'Already arranged, sir. All your meals have been arranged.'

That, Bodie figured, would be Ruby.

Nothing left to chance. He was missing her already.

He sat a while later after the coffee had been delivered and stared out the window, watching the landscape speed by. He found himself hoping all this wasn't going to turn out to be a waste of time. If Jasmine Soong had been kidnapped, it warranted the question why. For ransom? Her father was extremely wealthy and would be ready to pay for her return. Yet there had not been any demands.

Another possibility crossed his mind: kidnapped by a group who wanted her to sell to the highest bidder. Not a pleasant prospect, but Bodie had to look at that. If that was the case, she might already be out of the country. A captive on a ship taking her . . . where? The thought was not one Bodie wanted to consider. But he had to.

Through the trip, Bodie's mind ran through the permutations. He ate, he slept, and he tried to stay positive.

* * *

Henry Lee showed up on time. He walked into the hotel, picked out Bodie, and crossed to greet him. Lee was smartly dressed in a light gray suit, cream shirt and a black string tie. A good-looking Chinese man in his late twenties, lean and fit.

'I hope I haven't kept you waiting, Mr. Bodie,' he said. His English was perfect.

'Right on time. And let's forget the 'Mister.' The name's Bodie.'

'Then I'm Henry.'

Lee had a buff folder in his hands. He handed it to Bodie. Inside were neatly documented details about Jasmine Soong, even down to studio images of the young woman. Lee watched closely as Bodie read through the details. As well as Jasmine, there was information about Chin Yi Soong's business in San Francisco, and his associates and friends. Soong ran a very wealthy organization, with numerous businesses in and around the city. From what he read, Bodie saw he was respected, dealt fairly, and had no apparent enemies.

'Apparent' being the word. With so much wealth, it was entirely possible there was discontent somewhere along the line.

Lee waited patiently while Bodie studied the documents, finally raising his head to look at the young man. 'You put all this together?'

'Yes.'

'Well done, Lee. It must have taken you some time.'

'For Mr. Soong, nothing's too much trouble. I only hope it might be of help.'

'Jasmine doesn't strike me as the kind of woman to put herself at risk.'

'She isn't. Whatever happened to her wasn't caused because she did something foolish. The day it happened, she was simply taking in the sights, accompanied by a female chaperone and a guide named Jiang Chi. He was only slightly hurt; but young woman with her is still recovering from being struck down when the kidnapping happened. She is uncon-scious.'

'This Jiang Chi? He offer any useful information?'

Lee shook his head, and Bodie noticed the worry in his eyes. 'Li claimed he saw nothing that would help.'

'You don't believe him?'

'I have my doubts. Nothing more.'

'We'll keep that in mind,' Bodie said. 'Now, you mentioned the Tong in your report. Any particular reason?'

'How much do you know about them?'

'Not much. Only that they're a pretty hard bunch. Why don't you tell me about them.'

Henry Lee had enough detail to be able to explain how the Tongs had grown to become a powerful criminal organiza-tion that dealt in protection rackets, drugs, theft, even murder. They used intimida-tion to get what they wanted. The Tong was a secretive and dangerous group, not to be considered lightly. For Bodie, the most interesting part was when Lee spoke about the Tong and their involvement in prostitution and human trafficking.

'The Tongs also deal in the buying and selling of young women. Unfortunately, there's a market for such things.'

'Doesn't the law do anything?'

'The law does what it can, but like all official agencies, it's hampered by regulations and the need for public assistance. The police down here in Chinatown will receive no help from the people because of distrust of the gweilo — foreigners; and there is also the fear of reprisals against them. The Tong can be extremely vindictive. They have their own lawyers and the contrivance of outsiders who work for the Tong. Mr. Bodie, you'll find things difficult.'

'Well I wasn't expecting a flower parade.'

'What do you need?'

'Anything. A pointer. Somewhere for me to start, and if you're up to it, a guide.'

'Then we need to go to Chinatown. It's where Jasmine disappeared.'

'Then I'm in your hands, Henry Lee.'

Before they left the hotel, Bodie made a visit to his room, where he took his Colt Peacemaker and tucked it behind his belt, covered by his coat. He dropped a handful of extra cartridges into his pocket. The feel of the pistol nestling against his backbone was a comforting sensation. Picking up his hat, Bodie returned to the lobby, where Henry Lee was waiting.

'You armed?' Bodie asked.

'No. Should I be?'

Bodie managed a smile. 'Just curious, is all.'

'I have a feeling you'll have adequate protection for us both.'

'You got that right.

Bodie's precautions served them well. He never went into an unknown situation without being prepared. Finding out things were turning bad was not a time to wish he had anticipated the possibility.

# 3

Chinatown bustled with activity. Colorful and noisy, it teemed with crowds of Chinese and a sprinkling of Occidentals. The sounds and the smells were overwhelming — some pleasant, others not so. There was no avoiding the feeling of being in a totally different world. Street banners, colorful and adorned with Chinese symbols, hung from the sides of the buildings and even across the street. Street vendors hawked all kinds if exotic food, the rich aromas drifting back and forth. Bodie's experience of Chinese culture was limited to the people he had met out west, where they were primarily involved in menial occupations. He would have admitted to having little contact with them, though he saw them as hard-working reclusive people who kept to their own kind and appeared to have reserved, polite manners. Here they were active and seemed to have a propensity for talking.

'What do you think?' Lee asked, a slight smile on his face.

'Interesting. Is it always so busy?'

'Well — it's Chinatown.'

Bodie didn't noice he was drawing plenty of attention. The indifference in their faces made it hard to read what they might be thinking. Lee kept up a steady narration, pointing out various places and keeping Bodie advised of local high spots.

'We heading for anyplace in particular?' Bodie asked.

'There's someone I know who has little love for the Tong. In the past he suffered at their hands, and he has a need for a way to hit back at them. His name is Li Hung. A clever and resourceful man.'

★   ★   ★

'You'll take tea with me?' Hung said.

It was more a made decision rather

than a request. Henry Lee had advised Bodie of the need to follow tradition before they arrived at the herb and spice store Li Hung owned. The interior of the cramped space was heavy with the overpowering scents. Bodie had no idea what they were.

Lee had told Bodie that Hung was an old man who had defied the Tong when they had attempted to coerce him into paying protection money. More than once, enforcers had come to his store, and the old man had fought against them with a ferocity that drew respect from the Tong Masters. His total defiance of the younger Tong soldiers, allied with his skill using ancient Chinese martial arts that had not been witnessed for many years, had given the Tong cause to step back and leave him alone. The act was something very seldom practiced by the Tong. It was down to respect for Hung's age and his unflinching defiance.

Bodie had been surprised when he met Li Hung. He had expected an old man; but seeing the small stooped figure standing in the store, he felt he had been misinformed there. Hung, lean and wiry, his brown face lined beneath his cap of still-black hair, didn't seem capable of raising a hand to defend himself. From what Lee had told him, though, that was not the case. The old man's eyes flitted back and forth as he smiled at his guests, dwarfed by Bodie's towering presence.

At the rear of the store, the old man's living quarters were small but neat. Hung gestured for them to sit at the single table, then moved to a small stove where he prepared tea. It was served in fragile cups Bodie felt sure would break in his hand.

'So, Henry Lee, you have come seek my assistance.'

'Master Hung, I've brought my friend Bodie because he's looking for a young woman we believe has been abducted by — '

' — the Tong,' the old man finished. 'I had heard of this. Mr. Bodie, you have a special interest in this person?'

'Her family lives in New York. Her father has business interests there and here in San Francisco. He's wealthy and has influence. I've been asked to search for the woman. I admit I'm not familiar with the Tongs, so I'd be grateful for any help you might be able to offer, sir.'

'I find the Tong practice of dealing in the evil of trafficking a most distasteful crime — if that's what this is,' Hung said. 'I will try to find out who was involved.'

'I'm most grateful, Master Hung,' Lee said.

'Your help will be gratefully received,' Bodie added.

'My only connection to the criminal act is the man employed to show Miss Soong around Chinatown,' Lee said. 'He's called Jiang Chi.'

'If you return this evening, I will hopefully have some information for you. I know of this man.' The old man watched Bodie taste the tea, nodding his approval. 'It's to your liking?'

'Good, though not something I'm used to. Coffee would be my preference.'

'Ah yes, your American beverage. Each to his own. And you, Henry Lee — how is your family?'

'They're well, Master Hung.'

Hung nodded to himself. 'Then we should proceed with what we have to do,' he said. 'I will endeavor to find information for you. In the meantime, you may do well to visit to the one called Jiang Chi. When I heard about what happened, I asked questions. I have learned Chi has some connection to the Tong. I will seek to find out more.'

The little old man, in his black pants and tunic, saw them out of the store, where they paused for a moment.

'Could be a long day,' Bodie pointed out. 'If Hung suspects this Chi has Tong connections, the sooner we find him the better. Henry, it might be worth a visit to talk with this feller.'

'I didn't know he had links to the

Tong. That has come as a surprise to me. He was employed to guide Jasmine through Chinatown when she expressed an interest in the area. If I'd known about this, perhaps the kidnapping might have been prevented.'

'If kidnapping was the object. Whoever's behind it would have managed it one way or another.'

'Possibly so.'

'So what else do you know about this Jiang Chi?'

'Not a great deal. Except I do know where he lives.'

'Let's go and see what he has to say for himself.'

\*   \*   \*

Lee took Bodie through a maze of close alleys. He walked with the confidence of a man who knew exactly where he was going. Bodie had no idea. He was surrounded by Chinese, pushing his way through the crowds, with buildings teeming with people on either side. He felt hemmed in. Not nervous, just crowded. In his normal habitat, he could ride for days and not see a soul, with empty landscapes and a big wide sky above him. Here in the city, the rise of buildings near enough blocked out the sky. At some point Lee paused.

'Jiang Chi lives there,' he said. He indicated an alley across the street. As they stepped inside, the narrow passage muted the street sounds. Lee pointed to wooden stairs leading to the upper floor. 'Up there.'

Falling in behind his guide, Bodie slipped his hand under his coat and gripped the Colt. They reached the head of the stairs. Bodie heard Lee utter a warning sound. He raised a hand. Glancing by him, Bodie saw the door ahead of them standing ajar. From the other side of the door, they could hear a soft trail of sound.

'Get behind me,' Bodie said. He pulled his pistol into view, dogging back the hammer. Leaning forward, he gently pushed at the door. It swung wide, hinges creaking. Light fell across the floor inside. Bodie moved forward, eyes searching ahead of him.

He saw the blood-soaked figure stretched out on the bare boards, moving slightly. Blood was spreading out from the body, already a wide pool, expanding and partially staining the floorboards. The sound they had heard came from the man on the floor. His dying breaths. His movements ceased as Bodie and Lee neared him.

'Lee?'

'It's Jiang Chi.' The young man stood at Bodie's side. 'Tong work. Making sure Jiang Chi doesn't speak to anyone about what happened and where Jasmine Soong is.'

He crossed the room and knelt at Jiang Chi's side. Bodie heard the shocked gasp he expressed when he saw what had been done to the man.

Bodie looked down at Chi. Someone expert with a knife had sliced off the man's lips. Had shredded his tunic and cut his torso open. Bloody entrails had slithered out and lay in a glistening heap on the floor. The right hand, Bodie could see, was missing every finger and thumb. They lay in the pooling blood.

'A warning,' Lee said. 'To anyone thinking of interfering with Tong business. Jiang Chi might have helped Tung kidnap Jasmine, but he was not a true Tong, so they could not trust his silence. This serves as a reason why not to treat the Tong lightly. They don't tolerate outsiders.'

'Why am I getting the feeling this was directed at me?'

'Because your presence is known. That you're looking for Miss Soong. I only wish to make you understand how the Tong operates. No second chances. Once you go against them, there's no walking away.'

'Lee, these people don't know me. If they did . . . '

Lee smiled. 'They would understand you are a man who doesn't like to be warned off.'

'Feller, I knew we'd get along.'

'This may help, or not,' Lee said. 'Jiang Chi frequented a saloon along the waterfront. It's called The Golden Palace. On the fringe of the Barbary Coast district.'

Bodie had heard of the Barbary Coast. A dubious section of the city with a disreputable image. It catered to all the vices known to man and was no place to enter if a man wanted to remain safe. Bodie knew a number of towns in the west that could match its reputation.

' . . . so it should be visited with care.'

'I'll try and remember that.'

'You'll go there?'

'Sometimes a problem needs poking with a big stick to find out just how big it is.'

# 4

The Golden Palace showed a tarnished, gaudy front. Once-bright paint and gilded windows were starting to present their age. Bodie had found it easily, following Henry Lee's accurate directions, and now stood across the street studying the establishment. He could hear the noise emanating through the swing doors. A steady stream of men came and went. Bodie eased the Colt tucked in his belt under his coat and weighed up his options. It took him no time at all to realize he actually had none. If he wanted to find out anything, he was going to need to go inside the place; and if that was the case, he might as well do it now.

He had parted company with Henry Lee so the younger man could pursue some inquiries of his own that might go better if he were alone rather than in the company of a tall Gweilo. Racial distrust worked both sides of the trail, Bodie realized, in the same way as Bodie stepping inside The Golden Palace without Lee at his side might look less suspicious. Bodie was still debating the thought when he pushed the swing doors open and walked into the saloon.

His entrance didn't attract too much attention from the crowd of men at the bar and the scattering of tables. Sawdust covered the rough plank floor. There were a half dozen brightly dressed women moving around and doing their best to entice interest. That was to be expected. The women were employed to up the sale of liquor using their sometimes too-obvious charms.

He bellied up to the bar and ordered himself a beer, then scanned the big room, receiving curious glances from the men at the tables. His well-dressed appearance drew close inspection. It didn't bother Bodie at all. His only concern was to gain some interest other than his dress sense.

There was only the one bartender: a skinny prematurely bald man in a striped shirt and a wrinkled apron tied high above his waist. He placed Bodie's beer in front of him. 'New in town?'

Bodie nodded and asked in a voice that carried, 'Looking for a feller. Chinese. Name of Jiang Chi. Was told he sometimes comes here.'

The bartender shook his head. 'We get the odd one from time to time. Don't recall that name though.'

Bodie took a swallow from the beer glass. He heard a murmur of voices to his left and glanced into the big mirror behind the bar. Three men in a close group were looking his way and not doing much of a job hiding it. One of them, obviously the leader, was a big man, wide-shouldered and muscled, a tobacco-stained drooping mustache hanging over his mouth. His bull neck strained the collar of his shirt, and he was paying attention now Bodie had given Jiang Chi's name. It was a result be had been hoping for.

He did his best to ignore the man; yet even as he did, he was telling himself he wasn't going to go away. The man proved that by slamming down his glass and spilling beer on the bar. He pushed aside people in his path until he was facing Bodie.

'Something I can do for you?' Bodie said.

'Yeah, how about dying?'

If the threat hadn't been halfway serious, Bodie would have burst out laughing. 'Friend, I don't know what's gotten you riled, but is it worth getting yourself hurt over?'

The man laughed in Bodie's face, expelling beery breath.

'You going to put me to sleep?' the manhunter said. ''Cause your breath is purely liable to do just that on its own.'

'I'm goin' to crush you. You ask questions you shouldn't.'

The bartender said, 'Take it easy, Bennett. No trouble today, huh?'

'Mind your business, Rickman. Unless you want some of the same.'

'Take the man's advice, feller,' Bodie suggested. 'This dumb yahoo is interested in me for some reason. Maybe 'cause I mentioned Jiang Chi, though I doubt he could even spell the name.'

Bennett stared at Bodie for a few seconds. It was plain to see he wasn't used to being talked down to. He used his formidable presence to force others to step back, most likely to intimidate. Only this time he was facing a man who refused to back down.

Interest had risen as the group around Bennett began to anticipate what they had seen before. There was a degree of nudging each other, and vacuous grins forming as they saw their champion working his game.

'You want to dance with me, bucko?' Bennett said. His big fists formed at his sides and he took a short step forward. 'You really do?'

A sly grin formed beneath Bennett's drooping mustache. The fingers of his left hand, resting on the bar, were tapping with a nervous twitch. He brushed against a half-filled bottle of whiskey and snatched it up. His eyes never left Bodie's face as he brought the bottle to his mouth and took a long swallow. Then he banged the bottle back down on the bar and it toppled sideways, the whiskey glugging as it ran out and spilled across the bar top. The man seemed to find this funny and chuckled, his voice deep and gravelly.

'Hey,' the bartender protested.

'I told you once to mind your business, Rickman.' Turning back to face Bodie, Bennett pointed to the spilled whiskey. 'That's going to be your guts, bucko. Spreadin' across the floor.'

*He's a talker*, Bodie thought. *Likes to brag about what he's going to do.* The talk was supposed to unnerve the man's opponent. Throw him off his stride. Well, not this country boy.

'You like that, bucko? Hearin' what I'm going to do to you?'

'You mean talk me to death? That the best you Frisco assholes can do?'

Bennett reacted by letting go a harsh yell, whiskey breath blowing from his lips. He lunged forward, big hands clenching into bigger fists as he closed in on Bodie. There was little finesse in Bennett's move. He was no skilled fighter; simply an uncoordinated brawler who used his bulk and obvious strength to put his victims down. Right now he was expecting to smash Bodie to the saloon floor and most likely stomp him.

The manhunter stood his ground until the final moment, then launched a powerful fist that hammered Bennett's large gut. The sound of the landing blow was clearly audible to the gathering. Bennett stopped in his tracks, eyes opening wide, his jaw dropping. While the man was still frozen to the spot, Bodie hit him again, a left and a right to Bennett's heavy jaw. Bennett's head snapped back and forth, a spew of blood spraying from his torn lips and staining his thick mustache. For a moment, he rocked back on his heels. Bodie saw straightaway his blows were not about to put

Bennett down. The man was harder than he looked. Bodie drew back his right to land another punch, but Bennett reacted faster than anticipated. His left hand shot forward, catching Bodie's fist and stopping it in mid-flight. Bennett's bloody mouth formed a wider grin as he brought his own clenched fist across and clouted Bodie across the side of the head. The power behind the punch slid Bodie along the bar, sending bottles and glasses flying. He heard Bennett growl something, and as he turned, he saw the big man looming over him, hands reaching to grab him.

It flashed through Bodie's mind that he needed to end this fast. Bennett might have lacked the finer points of the pugilistic art, but in its place he had brute strength and a killing instinct. He would be able to take punishment and still keep coming back for more unless Bodie put him down hard.

With the man's bulk looming above him, Bodie pushed himself away from the bar, sliding beneath Bennett's grasp. He caught hold of the man's thick hair, his big hand palming against the back of Bennett's skull. Bodie applied every ounce of his own strength and rammed Bennett's head down hard against the thick edge of the bar. The thump could be heard across the saloon. Bodie repeated the move, hauling Bennett away from the bar and slamming him down again ... and again ... and kept doing it as he felt Bennett start to sag. There was no pity in Bodie's move. Bennett had initiated the conflict; Bodie was determined to end it.

When Bennett's legs loosened and he slid floorwards, Bodie stepped back. The big man hit the saloon floor with a heavy thud and lay still.

Bodie stepped back, reaching for the Colt under his coat, prepared to draw if anyone decided to continue Bennett's play. No one moved. A heavy silence had fallen. Bodie leaned against the bar. He could see a dent in the edge of it, slick with Bennett's blood. When he glanced down, he could see Bennett's broad back rising and falling with his breathing. Bodie wasn't sure how he felt about that. He hadn't killed the man — but Bennett still alive might present him with a problem in the near future.

'You up to hearing some advice?' Rickman, the bartender, said.

'Depends.'

'Just watch your back, friend. Bennett runs with a hard crowd.'

'I'll remember that.' He turned to face the crowd, sensing some hostility in the faces. 'We done here?' he asked. 'Anyone else want to upset my drinking time?'

There were no takers. Bodie could hear some mumblings in the crowd, but nothing happened. He turned and picked up his glass, taking a long swallow. His knuckles ached from hitting Bennett. He raised his eyes and stared into the big mirror hung behind the bar, seeing a bruise on his head where Bennett had landed his hard blow. He also picked out two of the men who had been standing close to Bennett. They were edging through the crowd on a line that would take them out the door. If they were intent on a quiet exit, they were not doing a very good job.

'Might be a wise move to finish your drink and leave,' Rickman said quietly. 'Bennett isn't the forgiving kind, if you know what I mean.'

'Friend, I've never walked away from a fight in my life. Too damn old to start doing it now.' He glanced down at Bennett's still form. 'I don't figure he'll be getting up for a while.'

The bartender had to smile. 'I'll say one thing in your favor, mister. You don't scare easy.'

Bodie pushed his empty glass across the bar. Rickman refilled it and took his money. 'You always this busy?'

'Friend, this is Frisco. Plain to see you're a newcomer. This town is always busy. We got people arriving every day. They come in by ship from every compass point. By train. On horseback. Some simply walk into town. They come for the California goldfields. Not that there's much left these days. The big strikes are over. Others are looking for business opportunities. You step out on the street and you'll see most every nationality there is.'

'I already did. Seen a lot of Chinese especially.'

'Where there's business, you'll find the Orientals.'

'Not so much in here. I'm still looking for this Jiang Chi?'

'There's one Chinese man who comes in and always mixes with Bennett and his pals. Never caught his name. That bunch is always up to no good. Tough crowd. Talk is they do work for the Tong.'

'I heard word about something called the Tongs,' Bodie said. 'Don't know much about them apart they run things in the Chinese community.'

'Best to stay well away, friend, because the Tongs play hard. They're a closed society. You don't want to get involved, 'less you want a knife between the shoulders.'

'Hell, I can do without that. Thing is I heard about them and got curious, is all. Sounds like good advice to steer clear. Thanks for the warning . . . ?'

'Stan Rickman.'

'Bodie.'

'From your accent, I'd say you're not from these parts.'

'Out west, mainly.'

'Long way from home.'

'Home? Can't say I could pin down anywhere as permanent. I move around a deal.'

Rickman simply nodded. He didn't question Bodie anymore. It was an unwritten rule not to ask too much about a man's personal business. If a man offered the information, that was fine, but it was beyond the remit for anyone to probe too deeply.

And Bodie was not going to say too much. Rickman seemed harmless enough; just a bartender talking to a customer.

Yet there was always the chance he might pass any information along to less than friendly ears. For all Bodie knew the bartender might be earning himself money on the side by doing just that. If that were the case, then Rickman was going to show a friendly face as he took in anything that might be of use to him. It was a sad state of affairs when a man had to judge who was to be trusted and who was conspiring to cheat on him. Bodie had been doing that for a long time. It was why he had stayed alive for so long.

He was new to San Francisco. There was no one in the city he could depend on, apart from Henry Lee. It meant, like so many times in the past, he was going to have to work on instinct. On his own nature.

Bodie finished his beer, slid the glass across the bar, and nodded to Rickman. 'Be seeing you, Stan. Grateful for the beer — and the advice.'

He turned and left the bar, stepping outside and heading in the general direction of his hotel. It was early afternoon, and the weather was pleasantly warm. There was a slight breath of air coming in off the water, bringing a salty tang of the ocean with it. Bodie walked steadily, taking in the sounds and the sights of the city. It was true what they said about San Francisco — it had to be the busiest place he'd ever seen. It made some of the towns he'd seen out west look as if they'd been deserted. Here the sidewalks and the streets teemed with people. Right at that moment, Bodie could have happily exchanged the place for a quiet town like Tombstone.

Apart from finding out that the man called Bennett had known Jiang Chi, he hadn't gained a great deal. He recalled Bennett's friends leaving the saloon and wondered what they might be up to.

It was a question he found the answer to quicker than anticipated.

And that was when he felt the unwelcome pressure of a gun muzzle being jammed against his spine. Who-ever was holding the weapon made a hard point of putting pressure on it to make certain Bodie got the message.

# 5

'Up ahead, friend, then take the alley there. If I have to, I'll shoot you right here on the street. Try me and it'll be the last thing you ever do. I won't kill you but make sure you never walk again.'

Bodie stayed silent, considering his next move. There was little he could do with that gun pressed against his backbone. No matter how fast he was, the man behind him would most likely be faster. All it took was a slight pressure on the trigger, and even Bodie's speed would be no match for a bullet. So he did as he was told, stepping into the mouth of the alley, where the walls on either side shut off some of the street sounds. Ahead of him, it stretched out to a dead end blocked by stacked wooden crates and barrels.

There was a second man waiting. Bodie recognized him as one of the pair who had been with Bennett in the bar. A set-up.

If Bennett had succeeded in putting Bodie down, the pair would not have been needed. If nothing else, it told Bodie he had already stirred up interest. His question about Jiang Chi had caused a reaction. Not quite the kind he had been expecting, but it proved there was more to the disappearance of Jasmine Soong than he'd thought earlier.

The man ahead of Bodie had a lean face that caused his facial bones to stand out. He wore a wool cap pulled down over his ears. His hands were down at his sides, pressed in against the rough material of the dark pants he wore, though not enough to conceal the knife in his right hand.

A gun . . . now a knife, Bodie thought. These yahoos were determined to earn their pay. 'I figure it's not my money you're after,' he said.

'You got that right,' the knife man said. His voice was quiet, almost pleasant. 'But we might take it anyhow. Like a bonus. And we'll add on what you did to Bennett. He's a good friend.'

'A friend? You picked the wrong kind of company, feller.'

'Huh?'

'The losing kind.'

'You want me to shoot this bastard right now?' the gunman asked.

'No. I want to stick him in the gut and watch him squirm some before he dies. Now you let me have him, Vic.'

'I don't like having to say it, but we got ya,' Vic said.

Bodie wasn't ready to disappoint him as long as the muzzle of the gun was still prodding his back. Doing something heroic sometimes needed a helping hand.

'You watch that damn hogleg,' the knifeman said. 'Shoot him that close a slug could go right through and hit me as well.'

'Jesus, Pardee, I ain't stupid.'

'Let's not take a vote on that.'

'Yeah? Fine, if you're going to be snippy about it.' The tone of the man's voice held a trace of annoyance.

Bodie felt the gun muzzle move away from his spine. Out the corner of his eye, he saw the shadow of the man holding it move to one side. Vic's arm revealed the silhouette showing the extended outline of the revolver he was holding.

'Do it, Pardee, before I change my goddamn mind. We don't want to mess this up. The Chinaman wouldn't be very happy about that.'

Pardee offered an anticipatory grin that showed his dull teeth. The knife in his hand moved from side to side as he stepped forward.

The seconds were slipping away. Bodie knew he was going to have to make his play now — and he did just that, hoping Vic had moved his gun far enough clear. He turned quickly, full circle anti-clockwise, the move bringing him round so that his right elbow swept up and across, smashing into the side of Vic's face full force. The man grunted as the unrestrained blow racked his jaw and sent it out of line. The pain momentarily paralyzed the man, allowing Bodie the chance to grasp Vic's gun hand, slipping his finger across Vic's where it lay against the trigger.

Pardee yelled, lunging forward to close the gap. Bodie angled the pistol and pulled back on the trigger, felt the weapon jerk as it fired. The .45 slug ripped into Pardee's hand, tearing away two of his fingers in a bloody spray. The knife spun from his grip, leaving Pardee staring at his mutilated hand before he started to scream.

Bodie jerked the pistol out of Vic's hand, dogging the hammer back again as he turned, pushed the muzzle under Vic's chin, and triggered a shot that ripped up through the man's head and took out a chunk of skull on its exit. Vic made no sound as he toppled back and slammed to the ground.

Turning about, Bodie held the gun

on the moaning Pardee. The man gripped his mutilated hand, staring at the bloody stumps of his missing fingers. 'Sonofabitch,' he said.

'Play rough and you take the pain.'

'This ain't finished,' Pardee said. He dragged a crumpled kerchief from his pocket and bound it around his hand. 'You walked into something you shouldn't have.'

'Story of my life.'

Movement at the head of the alley caught Bodie's attention. Curious onlookers were crowding together. Bodie heard authoritative voices demanding to be let through, and saw the long coats the of the two San Francisco police officers who stepped into view.

'Now what the hell is goin' on here?' The voice was powerful and held a strong Irish accent. 'Holy Mother, it's a slaughterhouse I see.'

The man was big and burly, his companion leaner. His face was red and full and round beneath the peaked cap he wore, and his powerful girth strained the seams of his uniform coat. A sturdy wooden club was clutched in his right hand. He fixed his eyes on Bodie's motionless figure. 'Is this down to you?'

'Self-defense,' Bodie said. 'They came at me so I defended myself. Is that a crime in San Francisco?'

'We'll see about that, boyo. Until then, you'd better hand over that weapon and come with me.'

'What about me?' Pardee wailed. 'He shot my hand to pieces.'

The big policeman glanced at him, recognition in his eyes. 'Pardee? Well, well, now, what have you been up to this time?'

'I done nothing. He shot me, Sergeant Kilpatrick.'

The second officer pointed at the knife Pardee had dropped. 'And I don't suppose that had anything to do with it?'

'Nothing except he was about to stick it in me,' Bodie said. 'The gun belonged to his partner. Had to take it off him before he used it.'

'He's lyin'. We was walking peaceable-like and he attacked us.'

'You were strollin' in the alley?' Kilpatrick said. 'You just happened to be holding a knife and this man came out nowhere and attacked you?'

'Somethin' like that,' Pardee mumbled.

Bodie reversed the pistol and handed it to the big policeman. 'He needs to see a doctor,' he said, indicating Pardee's bloody hand.

'Have the doctor look at Pardee's hand,' Kilpatrick told his partner. 'Then send someone down here to deal with the unfortunate departed. I'll be at the station with our friend here.'

After Pardee had been led away, Kilpatrick picked out a man from the crowd. 'Here, you, Jellicoe, go fetch a blanket to cover that mess up, then stay with him until help arrives.' As the man slipped away, Kilpatrick threw a warning glance at the onlookers. 'I know every face here. If there's any foolishness done about this body, I'll be lookin' for you. And you know I won't be joking about it.'

Kilpatrick glanced at Bodie, clearing his throat. 'Will you be walking with me to the station now? It's not that I don't believe your story, but I wouldn't be doing my duty if I failed to report what's happened here. You can have your say with Inspector Hallows. He's a fair man, and he might even be able to help.'

Bodie saw no profit in making his situation any more difficult, and admitted that a local police officer might be able to point him in the right direction. 'Why not,' he said, and followed as Kilpatrick led way out of the alley.

The walk to the local police office didn't take long. Despite his size, Kilpatrick moved quickly. He didn't say anything until they were clear of the area. 'I don't recognize your face. Sure enough, I'd say you were new to the city.'

'You got that right.'

'You talk like a westerner. Am I right?'

'Yeah.'

'And what is it that brings you all the way to our fair city?'

'Looking for someone. A missing person.'

'In Frisco? We got plenty of missing folk here, so it's luck to you, Mister . . . ?'

'Name's Bodie.'

'Well, Bodie my boy, you'll certainly be needing that luck.' Kilpatrick took a long look at him. 'Tell me, have you done this kind of thing before?'

'I do it for a living. Usually wanted men.'

'So it's a bounty man that you are?'

'This time it's not for a bounty. More for a friend. A favor.'

Bodie offered chapter and verse, including the finding of Jiang Chi's body. Kilpatrick listened without comment.

'This Ruby Keoh must be someone special to get you to come all this way.'

'Yeah, she is.'

'I hate to point it out, Bodie, but

there are a lot of folk in this city. How do you expect to find your Jasmine Soong?'

'That, Kilpatrick, is one hell of a question.'

'We'll have to see if we can help you with that, boyo. I don't take to the thought of some young woman being taken off the streets. Not at all.'

★   ★   ★

Inspector John Hallows looked to be in his late thirties, of medium height, fair-haired, and sporting a slim mustache, with good shoulders and a lean body. He listened to Kilpatrick's story in the office he inhabited as the senior inspector of the station. It had a window overlooking the street that allowed plenty of light through. When Kilpatrick finished, he withdrew, leaving Bodie alone with Hallows. The policeman poured coffee from an enamel pot on the stove in the corner of the room and handed one to Bodie before taking his place behind his plain wooden desk.

'It seems you're a long way from home, Mr. Bodie.'

Bodie managed a smile. 'You could say that.'

'Never been this far west before?'

'No.'

Hallows placed his coffee mug on the desk. He was silent for a few moments before he spoke.

'I hope you don't judge the whole of the city by what happened. San Francisco does have its peaceful side.'

'Seems I went and made myself known to the wrong people.'

'Finding this Jiang Chi murdered, and the way it happened, does suggest Tong involvement. They have unique ways of getting a message across. And Bennett and Pardee are names we know well. Vic Leeson too. They'll do most anything for the right amount of money. It's no secret they've done work for the Tong as well.'

'They started pushing,' Bodie said. 'And they wouldn't back off.'

'I can throw Bennett and Leeson in a cell; but apart from what they started with you, I don't have all that much to keep them for long.'

'Jiang Chi?'

'Little enough to go on there. I can have questions asked, but I can pretty well tell you we won't find anyone ready to talk. The Chinese community can be pretty closed-mouthed, and if there's Tong involvement we certainly shouldn't expect any kind of help.'

'I already figured the Chinese don't give out information too easy. I'm hoping Henry Lee has better luck.'

'We have to consider that Miss Soong might not still be in the city.'

'I know that, but as long as I don't have any other way to go . . . '

'You look like a man hoping for miracles.'

Bodie had to agree. For the moment, without much else to go on, he was wondering if Henry Lee might have better news.

A knock on the office door alerted

73

Hallows. A constable brought him a request from downstairs that took him away, with a quick apology for Bodie. 'Let me deal with this, then we can talk more. I doubt it'll take long. Help yourself to more coffee.'

Bodie did just that. He stood at the window and watched San Francisco go about its business, and not for the first time wondered where Jasmine Yi Soong was. Here he was in a big city, and at the moment he was no nearer to finding the young woman than he had been when he had stepped down off the train that brought him here.

*Okay, Bodie, stop acting like a damn novice. You've tracked men across the wilderness with less information.*

He heard the door open, and Hallows's voice. Then someone said, 'What the hell are you doing in San Francisco, Bodie?'

Bodie turned around and faced Jason Brand across the office.

# 6

A while earlier, Jason Brand had paused outside the telegraph office and reread the message he had just picked up. It had been sent by Frank McCord, his boss in Washington. In his usual brief and to-the-point manner, McCord had laid it on the line for his top operative.

'No additional information apart from what you already know. Find him. Stop him. McCord.'

Brand stared at the words, digesting them slowly. McCord made it all sound easy the way he said it.

He folded the buff slip and tucked it away in his coat pocket, then took a slow look around at the busy street and decided McCord was expecting some kind of miracle. He didn't believe he was going to find many of those in San Francisco, so he was going to have to depend on tapping into local knowledge, in this case the police. If anyone would have that kind of information, it would be San Francisco's finest. Brand needed a way in. A starting point. Who better than the local law?

He made some inquiries and found himself being guided to the San Francisco police department offices by the driver of a horse-drawn cab. The trip took a slow ten minutes through the thronged street. Paying off the driver, Brand stood and looked over the building. He was a couple of blocks from the waterfront, with the beginning of Chinatown off to his right.

Brand made his way up the steps and into the building. It was larger than most law offices he was used to seeing. Most frontier towns contained simple marshal's or sheriff's offices — a single room for the lawman and deputies, with a three to four cell area in back. Here he found himself in an open office with a manned desk to the side and doors leading off. Polished wood gleamed under the light. Framed pictures decorated the walls, and a line of chairs was pushed against the wall. Brand caught sight of a uniformed man behind the reception desk.

'I help you, sir?'

'Pretty nice place you got here.'

'We like it.' The man, wearing sergeant's stripes on his sleeve, loomed over the long desk. He was tall, wide-shouldered and burly. Mutton-chop whiskers adorned his brown face. He placed large hands flat on the desk. It was obvious he wasn't in the mood for small talk.

'I need to see one of your senior officers, Sergeant. On an important matter.'

'Let me decide about that.'

'My name is Brand. Jason Brand. Sergeant, I've ridden a train all the way from Washington, D.C. to get here, and to be honest it hasn't left me in the best frame of mind. Take my word, you don't want to pass this off lightly. Just find me one of your inspectors, and I'll explain why I'm here to him.'

Brand's voice had a sudden hard edge to it. He held his gaze on the sergeant and refused to back down. The police officer stiffened, leaning forward as he made up his mind what to do. Then he turned abruptly and called out. The door to the office behind the desk opened and a thin-faced young officer showed.

'Pierce, go find Inspector Hallows. Ask him to come here immediately.' Pierce scuttled out of sight.

'You mind if I sit down, Sergeant?' Brand said quietly.

'If you've a mind.'

Brand dropped onto one of the chairs, stretching his long legs out. He was ready to get himself a meal. The food on the train had been less than the best; and the restaurant at his hotel, where he had simply left his bags, didn't open for a few hours.

'Mr. Brand? I'm Inspector Hallows. I'm told you need to speak to me on what appears to be an important matter that can't wait?'

'It can't. Let me mention a couple of things. The Tong. Opium. Kwai Fu Tung.'

'I'd like you to come up to my office, Mr. Brand. I have someone with me right now who will be as interested in what you have to say as I am.'

Brand followed the policeman up the stairs that led to a bare corridor. Hallows reached a door and pushed it open. 'This is turning out to be a strange day,' he said.

Brand stepped inside the office, took one look at the tall broad-shouldered figure standing at the window, and recognized him.

'What the hell are you doing in San Francisco, Bodie?'

Hallows took his place behind his desk, feeling even more confused than he had been a few minutes ago. Not only did he have two men with similar reasons for being in the city, but it seemed they already knew each other. Explanations were given that offered Hallows an insight into both men's reasons for ending up in San Francisco. It made him aware there was more going on than he might have imagined.

'Let me get this straight,' he said. 'It looks to me as if everything points to Tung. Bodie here is looking for Chin Yi Soong's daughter, while Mr. Brand has been assigned to locate this man Traeger. Now it appears Tung and Traeger may be involved in a scheme to force Soong to surrender control of his company to Tung in return for the safety of his daughter. I have to say that final thought is simply an assumption, but the way things are looking, it doesn't appear too fanciful.'

'I'd say that covers it,' Brand said.

'And neither of you two had any idea there might be a connection?'

'Not until we met up just now,' Bodie agreed.

Hallows pushed his coat open and hooked his thumbs in his vest. It was a habit he maintained when he was working things out in his mind. His gaze moved between Bodie and Brand. 'Traeger's intending to move up in the criminal world by joining up with Tung?'

'There's a thriving trade back east. It came to the notice of the Justice Department,' Brand said. 'Story goes he wants to tie up with the Tong and create a new alliance. My assignment was to prevent that from happening. Plus he's wanted for the suspected murder of one of his money scheme victims.'

'As simple as that?'

Bodie chuckled softly. 'It won't be that simple. The more I think about it the closer it looks as if Jasmine's kidnap has to do with her father being forced into accepting Tung as a partner. His business has a lot of influence. Trade between east and west coasts. Good cover for a Tong smuggling in their contraband.'

Hallows shook his head in frustration. 'Hell's fire, this is getting beyond me. I'm just a policeman. I deal with local crime. That gives me enough headaches. Last thing I need is some kind of criminal conspiracy that operates coast to coast.'

'Like it or not, Inspector, it's heading your way,' Brand said. 'In fact, I think it's already here.'

Hallows glanced across the office to where Sergeant Kilpatrick was standing quietly by, listening to every word. He had brought the Irishman in to hear what was being said, valuing the man's opinion. 'What are you thinking, Seamus?'

Kilpatrick pursed his lips. 'In truth, Inspector, when you call me Seamus, we really must be in trouble. But from what these boys have been telling, our fair city could be heading for an almighty black brew. Now, we all understand the Tong. A nasty bunch always up to no good. And — beggin' your pardons, gents — if we don't move our asses and step on it, this mess is only going to get bigger and bloodier. The sooner we act, the better.'

Hallows held back from laughing out loud and simply showed a wide grin. 'I do believe you expressed what we're all feeling, Sergeant. I'll do my best to give you what help you may need, though I must confess to not really knowing what that's right at this moment.'

Brand caught Bodie's eye. The man-hunter inclined his head in silent acknowledgment.

'Inspector, I hope you're prepared for things to get a little hectic from here on in,' Bodie said. 'There's no way we can handle this without it getting very noisy. I can't see this Tung feller going down without a fight.'

Hallows expressed a deep sigh. 'Damned if I wasn't expecting you to say something like that. I'd prefer a quieter life, but I can only see that vanishing into the distance at a fair clip.'

'Inspector, you mind if Bodie and I have a break to talk all this over? Give ourselves a chance to compare notes. Once we have matters cleared up, we'll come back and sit down with you again.'

Hallows nodded. 'Go ahead. I'm up to my shoulders in other investigations. You two seem to have matters in hand.

Just remember I'll pitch in if and when you come to any decision. The last thing I need is for this to get out of control. So if you can figure how to calm things down, I'm all for it.'

As they walked out of the station, Bodie glanced at Brand. 'He did say calm things down, didn't he?'

Brand nodded. 'Thing is, he has no idea.'

'None at all,' Bodie agreed.

# 7

Captain Richard Hunt, a British government agent who was based in Jamaica, watched the two men emerging from the San Francisco police station. He had been on his way there himself, but the moment he recognized one of the tall figures, he changed direction and decided to follow them because he knew one of them well.

A wry smile edged the agent's lips. The last time he had encountered the American, Brand had ended up in a hospital bed in Yucatan, recovering from a near-fatal blow delivered by the Tong criminal, Kwo Han. The blow had not ended Brand's life, but had robbed him of his memory, leaving him with no recollection of who he was or why he was in Mexico. Later, Hunt had learned, Brand had vanished, ending up in Butte, Montana, involved in another violent affair that had resulted in his memory coming back but leaving him injured — which seemed to be a regular occurrence in his life. His involvement with that incident had also brought about his relationship with Virginia Maitland, and as far as Hunt knew, that was ongoing.

From the way Brand handled himself, Hunt guessed he was back on form; and if that was so, he had the feeling Brand was here in San Francisco on assignment. Hunt may have been wrong, but he could imagine Brand's presence having to do with Hunt's own reason for being in the city. If there had been time, Hunt would have telegraphed Frank McCord and asked why Brand was here. He felt, rightly or wrongly, it was too much of a coincidence Brand showing up here in the city by the bay.

* * *

They found a coffee house near the station and picked a table at the back.

At this time of day, the place was quiet. Brand lit a thin cigar from his pocket and leaned back.

'A surprise, but good to see you, Bodie.'

'Yeah. Now do you really expect things to get rowdy like last time?'

'Am I supposed to answer that?'

'I guess not.'

'I can tell you that peace and good-will to all don't follow this chap around,' someone said at Brand's elbow.

Brand looked up, suspicion on his face. The moment he recognized Richard Hunt, the expression vanished. 'Just who in hell is going to show up next?' he said, pushing to his feet and grasping Hunt's extended hand. 'Richard, you're off your home ground again. Last time it was Mexico.'

'You go where the orders send you.' Hunt smiled. 'You should know that better than anyone.'

'Where's Rumboy? He not with you?'

'He's keeping a watch back home in Jamaica.'

'I don't want to break you two apart,' Bodie said, 'but who the hell is Rumboy? And Jamaica?'

Hunt took a seat as Brand sat back down.

'Earlier assignment,' Brand said. 'I was following a trail of ex-Confederate gold. Took me to Yucatan, where I met Hunt.'

'It was, to say the least, an interesting time,' Hunt said.

'Interesting?' Brand was unable to prevent a grin forming. 'British understatement. I teamed up with this feller and ended up with my skull cracked from a Tong hatchet.'

Bodie stared at him. 'You say Tong?'

'Damn right. Son of a bitch called Kwo Han. Hit me so hard I lost my memory for a while.'

Bodie held up his hands. 'Whoa there. Let's go back a mite. Tongs? Just like we have here?'

'Kwo Han was running a Tong group from Yucatan. He'd taken a liking to the place,' Hunt said. 'I was on his tail because the Tong were expanding into the Caribbean — including Jamaica, where I was based. We had contraband being sent there by the Chinese, especially drugs like opium. My job was to track Han and put a stop to him. When Jason and I met, he was after Han because of the gold. Han was making a deal with a criminal organization based in the eastern US. It would have worked if we hadn't put a stop to Han's plan. Unfortunately, the opium trade has recently started up again, and it's become serious. Jamaica is one of the recipients of the damn stuff. As I had previous experience with the Tong, I was assigned to look into the business, which brought me here to San Francisco and your Kwai Fu Tung character.'

For Hunt's benefit, Brand related the background to his and Bodie's reasons for being in San Francisco.

'So we're more or less on the same trail here?' Bodie said. 'Milo Traeger. This Tung hombre. Jasmine Soong.'

'And the opium,' Brand said.

'Hell, working all this out could give a feller a headache.'

'So you believe Miss Soong was taken in order to force her father to work with Tung?' Hunt said.

'Chin Yi Soong has ships that carry merchandise along the coast. West to east. Cargo from San Francisco to New York. Tung would be able to move a lot of opium that way. The Tung-Traeger deal would work out favorably for them.'

Brand could almost see the wheels turning in Bodie's head.

'Connections,' the manhunter said.

'They'd have the means to get the opium to the east coast. Apart from selling to the Chinese community, opium has caught on with the regular public. It's become big business. It might not be strictly illegal, but there's a growing conflict between the Tongs, so Tung is making sure his supplies reach the east coast faster than any others. The competition is turning violent, and people are getting hurt, so there's a need to put a stop to it.'

'Shipping overland takes a long time,' Hunt said. 'And it's risky. By cargo ship, Tung shortens the time. And he'll be able to send large consignments, even ship them across the Caribbean.'

Brand caught the eye of the waitress to refill their coffee cups and bring one for Hunt. 'So they need a trusted company. One that makes regular trips between San Francisco and New York,' he said. 'They kidnap Chin Yi Soong's daughter to force him to work with them. His people deliver the opium as regular cargo, and Soong's ships run it around the coast to New York. Soong has no choice. He has to make sure the delivery's secure. He isn't going to do anything that might get his daughter harmed.'

'Smart deal. And Jasmine Soong is caught up in the middle as the means to force her father to cooperate.'

'You have any leads?'

'Been working on that.' Bodie explained about Henry Lee and his meeting with Li Hung. 'The old man said he'd do some checking, see if he could find out anything. Appears he's well respected in the Chinese community. He has no love for the Tong.'

'And your man Lee?'

'Same. Scouting out the area. Less chance of standing out. We're the wrong color and size. We start poking around and the Chinese will walk away. Lee might be able to find out things I couldn't.'

# 8

Henry Lee had not been as smart as he should have been. Though his intention had been to gain information that might help Bodie, Lee had not counted on Kwai Fu Tung having so many people on the streets. The Tong Master had not gained his reputation by being lax. He was, after all, one of the city's leading criminals, and would have his eyes and ears all around. Lee had told Bodie he would search out for any information that would help him. He was as discreet as possible, but once he began to ask questions he should have realized his interest would be reported to Tung. To be fair to himself, Lee admitted he was no experienced Tong soldier, but simply an ordinary citizen of San Francisco who worked for a businessman.

By the time he realized he was being

watched himself, it was too late. Despite becoming nervous, Lee continued his search. He owed it to Bodie, but even more he owed it to Chin Yi Soong, his employer. Soong had given Lee his job in the first place and made him a trusted employee. It was the least Lee could do for him. Soong's daughter was precious to him. Lee understood the concept of family loyalty. Chinese culture revolved in great part around family, so Lee felt obliged to do all he could to assist in trying to get her back.

He had picked up some slight information on Tung, and it led him in the direction of the waterfront, where he had learned about the warehouse Tung owned. Lee debated whether to turn around and report his findings to Bodie. The tall American would know how to handle it. He was still undecided when two Chinese fell into step beside him, one on each side, and a third moved up close behind. Lee felt the sharp prick of what he knew to be a knife blade press into his lower back.

'As you seem interested in Master Tung's business,' one of the men said, 'we'll take you to see him.'

When Lee hesitated, the man on his other side said, 'We insist.'

The knife pressed a little closer, and Lee knew he had no choice. He realized his position was not favorable. He also understood he had no say in the matter.

The Tung warehouse was large. Three stories high and stood on its own, with its frontage directly over the water. A series of wooden beams jutted out from access doors on each floor. An arrangement of ropes on pulleys would allow cargo to be hoisted directly from berthed cargo vessels to be pulled inside for storage. Lee's escorts led him inside the warehouse and up the wooden stairs accessing each floor. He was taken to the uppermost floor, where Kwai Fu Tung stood talking to his enforcer, Lo Keye. Tung waited until Lee was brought close. He looked Lee up and down.

'He dresses just like his Gweilo

master,' Keye said, his tone condescending. 'A little lap dog. We should finish him now. Waste no more time. While he still lives, he's a problem.'

Tung raised hand to silence his enforcer. 'I understand you've been asking many questions, Henry Lee,' Tung said. 'About me and my business. Why?'

'My employer's daughter has been kidnapped. Taken off the street. I'm certain you're involved. I want to know why.'

'The lap dog makes noise like a man,' Keye sneered.

'Tell me something, Henry Lee. Do you speak for this Gweilo who is also looking for this woman?' Tung seemed amused. 'We know this man Bodie is also looking. Please don't be so surprised. There's little in San Francisco I can't learn about. We even know where he's staying.'

'And you've been to speak with the old one,' Keye said. 'Li Hung.'

'Was it Hung who told you where to

find me?' Tung asked.

'No. I found you myself. It's not hard to pick up your smell.'

The vicious blow to the back of Lee's head knocked him to his knees. His senses spun. He had gone too far, allowing his feelings to get the better of him. He felt rough hands grab at him and haul him upright.

'You see,' Tung said, 'now I'm disappointed, Henry Lee. There we were, having a polite conversation, and you had to spoil it. All I wish to know is how much you might have found out about my business with Miss Soong and her father. For the moment, I wish it to be kept private. But with this American looking around . . . well, you must understand the need to maintain secrecy.'

'Then you have a problem, Tung. Whatever you've done will come out. Even you won't be able to stop that.'

'I agree about the problem. Chin Yi Soong may be in New York, but we can be sure he'll be looking for his daughter. He has the influence and the wealth to set up a search for her. It would be interesting to learn what he has found out. Knowing Soong's plans could help me.'

'Then I was right. You were responsible for kidnapping Jasmine Soong.'

'Very well. Yes, I arranged it. Not that the knowledge will be of any use to you.'

'Dead men can't give away secrets,' Keye said. He turned suddenly, his fists slamming against Lee's face, blood spurting from his mouth. The blows stunned Lee and he sagged in his captors' arms, letting his weight drag. His head fell forward in feigned unconsciousness, and he remained in the position.

'Now we must wait for him to wake,' Tung said impatiently. 'You must learn greater patience, Keye.'

Henry Lee kept up his pretense while he listened to what was being said. The enforcer stayed silent, aware of his position and not wanting to anger the

Tong Master. Finally he summoned courage to speak again.

'Master Tung, we do need to find out what this one has learned.'

'True,' Tung agreed.

'We could take him out to the Belker place, or on to *The Lily Wanderer* in Mora bay. All very quiet places. Even more remote than here.'

'I'm aware of that, Lo Keye. It's why we have Miss Soong on board. But I need answers from this man now.'

Keye could not fault Tung's reasoning. 'So shall I soften him up?'

'It would be a shame not to employ your talent for inflicting harm. But don't go too far. As you said yourself, a dead man is unable to talk.'

Henry Lee understood what was going to happen as the men holding him tightened their grip. He opened his eyes to see what was coming at him.

'So,' Tung laughed. 'I thought as much. It's foolish of you to try to deceive us. And it will do you no good. Lo Keye, practice your arts on this man.'

Lee saw Keye step in front of him, face set as he nodded to himself in preparation. When he did move, it was with frightening speed. Lee didn't even see the first blow coming — but he felt it as the hardened edge of Keye's hand slammed against his ribs. Pain flared as the impact severely bruised his muscles and bone. Not enough to cause permanent damage, but hard enough to cause him pain. The blow was followed by others, each delivered with force enough to make Lee cry out. Ribs. Torso. Against his upper arms that left Lee's limbs near paralyzed as the muscles were struck. A palm strike beneath his jaw, snapping his teeth together and making his gums bleed. More blows followed, impacting against his cheek, his mouth. A gash was opened over his left eye, blood streaming down his face. If Lee had not been held upright, he would have dropped to the floor.

'It's amazing the many moves Keye possesses,' Tung said. 'He can inflict much pain without killing you. Consider this, Henry Lee. I will allow you time to think about it. In the end it will be in your hands whether you wish to suffer more or tell me what I need to know. Before you die.' Tung gestured at the men holding Lee. 'Secure him, and we'll allow him to consider.'

Lee's captors dragged him across the room. In his painful condition, a single thought permeated his conscious thought. *If I don't get out of here, I'm a dead man. There's no way Tung will allow me to live.*

There was no doubt in his mind. Keye would turn him into a living corpse to get information from him. He had to break free somehow.

As the two men half-dragged him across the floor, a faint hope rose. Not only faint, but completely reckless. Lee almost smiled at the thought. Here he was, close to being killed, and he was worrying about acting recklessly.

The cause of his momentary concern was the tall wood-framed windows set in the end wall of the building. He knew from the layout that the rear wall of the warehouse looked out onto the water of the bay, and the windows were were at least two stories high. That would mean at least a twenty-five-foot drop. A fall from that height could easily kill him — and that was what brought him back to his earlier amusement.

He could die by Tung's hand — or by the impact of the fall. In the passing seconds, Lee decided he would prefer his death to come from a high fall rather than the prolonged suffering Tung and his men would inflict. Out of the corner of his eye, he saw that the closest window was no more than ten feet to his left. The dusty glass was held in place by thin wooden slats that were weathered and fragile, easy to break through. Or so he hoped — because that was his way out.

Once he had made his decision, Lee acted on it. He planted both feet hard on the timber floor, bringing himself and his escort to a sudden stop. His action caught the two men off guard. They had not been expecting any kind of resistance from their captive after his punishment by Keye. Their loose grip on Lee's arms was broken, and before they could grasp him again, he turned and broke into a run toward the closest window. Realization of what he was about to do sank in quickly, and the pair lunged forward, hands reaching out to recapture him.

They failed. Both were heavier and bulkier than the younger man; and as fast as they were, he stayed ahead of them. Sheer terror overtook him as he closed in on the window. Yet the feeling only made him move faster, throwing up his hands to cover his face as he launched himself forward. As his feet left the floor, he experienced a moment of self-doubt, but there was no turning back from what he had done.

He managed to twist his upper body, striking the center of the window with his left shoulder. There was no resistance. The weight behind his headlong dive took him through the frame and the shattering glass. His momentum threw him clear of the building, and he described a wide curve as he began to fall.

He had little time to do anything save draw in a deep breath before he hit the surface of the water and plunged headfirst down into the depths. He struggled to right himself as he sank, fighting to slow his descent. The water was chill, and it helped to clear his mind and clarify his thoughts.

He knew he had to reach the surface before the air burst from his lungs. Panic took over when he realized he had no idea which way around he was, until he twisted and saw the gleam of daylight overhead. The problem was, it appeared to be so far away that he was certain he would not be able to hold out until he reached it. He kicked with his legs and tried to work his arms, but they were still partially numbed from Kiang's brutal blows.

Despite his condition, he knew he

had to try. He had information now that would help Bodie in his search for Jasmine Soong. Somehow he had to get that information to him.

But the surface of the water still seemed to be too far away. Lee struggled to keep air in his lungs, even though they were starting to burn and the salt water was stinging his eyes . . .

★ ★ ★

'Do you see him?'

Keye turned from the shattered window and shook his head. He snapped harsh words at the two men who had allowed Lee to break free. The pair withdrew and started down the stairs leading to the bottom floor of the warehouse.

'We must hope the fall killed him,' Tung said. 'He could identify us if he survives and contacts the American. I don't want that to happen, Keye. I'll put you in charge of the search. Use the location of the hotel where this Bodie is staying. Lee may try to reach him. This time, if you find he's still alive, you must make sure he doesn't stay that way.'

★   ★   ★

Lee struck something in the murky green water, felt the slippery texture of wooden pilings, and realized he was under the dock. He kept contact with the encrusted timber, clawing his way to the surface and sucking in fresh air as his head emerged. He stayed there for some time, gripping the piling. He could feel the restless motion of the lapping water, staring around as he calmed himself. Now he could feel the pain in various parts of his body. It hurt when he breathed where Keye's blows had bruised his ribs. His arm muscles begged for relief. He felt the salt water stinging the cuts on his hands and face where glass had slashed at him as he crashed through the warehouse window. And his body ached from the brutal blows he'd received.

Lee consoled himself with the fact he was still alive. The reckless leap through the window had saved him. His body was bruised and battered from the fall, but he was lucky not to have broken any of his limbs. Now he needed to get himself clear of the area, because he knew without a doubt that Tung would have his people out searching for him. He needed to find Bodie and let him know about Tung and the Tong's involvement. Tung would be equally determined to stop Lee before he contacted the American.

Rested, Lee worked his way through the forest of pilings, his progress hampered by the swell and ebb of the water. His way took him under the waterfront structures, and eventually he found himself in shallower water where the sea bordered the land, and was able to wade ashore. Here he found a stretch of muddy flats. The smell of the detritus that washed up to the shore reminded him where he was. Flotsam rolled on the surface of the sea, human and natural. The air was tainted by the odor of fish and oil and waste food that had been discarded. Lee realized he could have ended up floating on the tide himself if his fall from the high window had not turned out well.

A curtain of fog drifted in from the bay and enveloped the shore. Lee was able to use it as he trudged his way from the wharf, carefully making his way inland. Once he left the seafront area behind, he was able to work his way through the side streets, away from the busier areas. He was still in some discomfort from his treatment by Tung's men and his progress was slow, but he was determined to pass along what he had found to Bodie.

When he reached the street where the hotel stood, he took a look around. He was receiving attention because of his bedraggled appearance. The cuts and bruises on his hands and face stood out. His face was streaked with blood, and he could understand why people were stepping around him, their faces showing their alarm.

Lee didn't pay any attention to that. He was more concerned as to whether any of Tung's people had seen him and followed him back to Bodie's hotel. He felt that would have been unfortunate. The last thing he wanted to do was draw attention to where Bodie was staying.

He paused on the sidewalk, turning to take a careful look around. That was when he saw a closed carriage swerving across the street in his direction. As it swung sideways on, he saw one of the side curtains ease open, and a hand holding a revolver appeared. Lee turned around in order to get clear.

The sound of the shot was loud. It startled passersby and alarmed horses on the street. Lee felt a hard blow to his left shoulder, then one to his body. The impact hurled him into the wall of the building he was passing. As the carriage sped by, a third shot caught him in the left arm, the slug passing though his limb and tearing a ragged hole in his coat on its exit. Lee staggered off balance, blood pulsing from the bullet wounds as he stumbled to his knees. A third shot put a slug in his chest, and Lee fell face down on the sidewalk, oblivious to the startled screams around him. His face scraped across the sidewalk.

By the time the carriage had turned the corner ahead, a crowd was gathering around Harry Lee — but by then he was unconscious and neither saw nor heard anything.

# 9

'I need to go look for Henry Lee,' Bodie said.

'It's a big city,' Hunt pointed out.

'I can find my way back to Li Hung's store. He'll help. We can join up at my hotel later.'

Bodie gave them the location.

'That's one of the best in San Francisco,' Hunt said.

'Seems my benefactors only go for the best.'

'I'll have a word with McCord,' Brand said. 'See if I can get him to spend a little more on my accommodation.'

They parted company, Brand and Hunt heading back to have a word with Inspector Hallows. They hadn't gone far before Brand glanced around, murmuring under his breath.

'What is it?'

'Couple of Chinese heading our way.'

'Jason, the place is full of Chinese.'

'They're not all carrying those damn hatchets the Tong seem to favor.'

The sight of the deadly blades brought back memories for Brand. A sandy beach in Mexico and the fight against Kwo Han and his men; the finale of that conflict had been the Tong leader's attack on Brand. The blur of steel as the hatchet crashed against his exposed skull and put him down a second after he had fired his final shot at Han. The hatchet blow that had taken Brand's memory and almost his life.

The shock of recall snapped Brand into action as he drew his Colt and pulled the trigger. The crack of the shot sent a .45 lead slug into the man. It thudded into his chest, coring in deep, and the Tong stumbled and went down hard, the hatchet bouncing from his grip.

From beneath his coat, Hunt pulled out an identical weapon. He had chosen the American pistol for his visit to the country, realizing there would be no problem getting hold of ammunition. And he admitted he liked the feel of the weapon and its power. He turned to face the second Chinese. The man moved with surprising agility, swerving to make himself a harder target. Hunt brought his pistol round, but was too slow to avoid contact as the Tong soldier lashed out. The keen edge of the hatchet sliced across his right arm, cutting down from his bicep and across his forearm. Hunt fell back, a shocked cry bursting from his lips. Despite the wound, he lashed out with his left arm, his fist connecting with the attacker's jaw, spinning him sideways. Before the Chinese could recover, Hunt braced his gun hand with his left, lifted the Colt and put a single shot through the side of the man's skull. The Chinese went down in a burst of blood and brains, slamming to the ground.

Brand reached the agent's side as Hunt clutched at his bloody arm. 'We need to get you to a doctor.'

'You aren't going to get any argument from me there, old chum,' Hunt said.

His face had drained of color and he was swaying on his feet. He let Brand support him as he waved at an empty horse-drawn cab. The driver might have argued at having a bleeding man in his vehicle, but the expression on Brand's face advised him not to.

'Nearest doctor, and make it fast.'

The driver pushed his horse through the streets at full speed, the vehicle rocking from side to side. When he brought it to a halt, Brand helped Hunt down.

'Doc Boyd's office,' the driver said. 'He's a good man.'

Brand got Hunt to the door and pushed it open. 'We need help here,' he called.

The man who stepped out the back room took one look at the bleeding mess of Hunt's arm and gestured behind him. 'Bring him through.'

Between them, they got Hunt onto the examination table, where the doctor bent to his task. He cut away Hunt's jacket and shirt, exposing the long, deep gash the hatchet had opened. By this time, Hunt had lapsed into unconsciousness.

'His name is Hunt. Richard Hunt.'

'Mr. Hunt has a nasty wound . . . I'm Nathan Boyd, by the way. Is this man a friend of yours?'

'Yeah. Doc, do what you can for him. He deserves the best.'

'And you are?' Boyd asked without pausing in his examination of the open bleeding wound.

'Jason Brand.'

Boyd crossed the room and pulled on a long white coat, then gathered instruments and medicines. 'How did this happen?'

'We tangled with a couple of Tong members,' Brand said, as if that was the only explanation required.

'I imagine you must have done something to upset them.'

'A little.'

'Should I be expecting a visit from them?'

'Not the ones we faced.'

Boyd glanced at him. 'Now that says a lot.'

'Doc, I don't want to put you in any danger from the Tong.'

'Danger? Mr. Brand, I've worked in Arizona and New Mexico and been shot at by Apache Indians, so I do understand danger. Believe me when I say working in San Francisco can sometimes be downright boring. That's why I offer my services to the police.'

'Dr. Boyd, I need to speak to them. I'll get back soon as I can.'

'There's a telephone in the other room. It may be a new invention, but even as primitive as it is, a connection to the police department is extremely useful. You can speak directly to the local station. Have you used a telephone before?'

'Enough to make the call. You know an Inspector Hallows?'

Boyd didn't look up this time from ministering to Hunt. 'I know John Hallows well. As I said, I do work for the police department.'

Brand left him to his patient and went to find the telephone and make his call.

# 10

Bodie saw the crowd gathered outside the building where Li Hung had his store. He had a bad feeling as he eased his way through, and it increased when he saw uniformed police officers stationed outside.

'You're not allowed inside,' one of the policemen said.

'Has something happened to Li Hung?'

'I'm afraid so,' a familiar voice said.

Sergeant Seamus Kilpatrick pushed his way through the crowd to confront Bodie.

'What . . . ?'

'Someone cut the old man up like a dead fish,' Kilpatrick said. 'No easy way to say it, Mr. Bodie.'

'He was only trying to help me.'

'I believe you're learning about the Tong the hard way, boyo.'

'I'm getting the urge to do something about them,' Bodie said. 'They don't seem to give damn about anyone who stands in their way.'

'Law unto themselves.'

'Kidnap. Murder. This Tung hombre needs his rope shortening. Stop him running wild.'

'You find your friend?' Kilpatrick asked. 'The young Chinese feller?'

'No.'

'I guess you'll be worried now,' the Irishman said as he and Bodie watched Li Hung's covered body being brought out and placed in a waiting buggy.

A uniformed constable came across to where they were standing. 'Message from Inspector Hallows, Sergeant. He says you need to locate a Mr. Bodie . . . '

'You've done that, feller,' Bodie said.

'Tell it, Johnson.'

'You need to go to Dr. Boyd's office. He had a patient brought in who identified himself as Henry Lee. The man's in a bad way. Badly beaten, and he's been shot.'

Kilpatrick dismissed the man. 'I have a police buggy across the street. It can get us there quickly.'

'Let's hope it's fast enough.'

Kilpatrick took the reins himself, urging the horse to a reckless speed through the city streets. It took them twenty minutes to reach the doctor's office. Bodie was out of the buggy before it came to a stop. He was at the door when Brand appeared, and the look on his face told Bodie all he needed to know.

'Sorry, Bodie. He died a few minutes ago. Doc Boyd did everything he could, but Henry was too badly injured.'

'Where is he?'

Brand led him through to the room at the rear where Henry Lee lay beneath a white sheet.

'Mr. Bodie,' Boyd apologized, 'I wish we had better news for you. He was found near your hotel and brought here as quickly as possible.'

Boyd drew back the sheet covering Lee. Bodie could see the livid bruising on the young man's flesh, and the cuts and abrasions, as well as the bullet wounds.

'I've only managed a cursory examination so far,' Boyd said. 'It appears he was severely beaten. Very severely. By someone who knew how to inflict pain. I believe a number of ribs had been broken. On top of that were the gunshot wounds. Your friend suffered greatly before he died. I'm surprised he was able to even talk.'

Bodie looked at the doctor. 'What about?'

'That he needed to speak with you because he had information you might find useful. He told me he'd found out where Jasmine Yi Soong was being held.'

'Where?'

'At a homestead outside the city,' Brand said from behind him. 'And there was something about a boat called *The Lily Wanderer.* Tung had her taken there to keep her secure.'

'Ain't a damn thing going to be

secure for Tung now,' Bodie said. 'He's brought this down on himself, and I aim to deliver it.'

'And I promised to help,' Inspector Hallows said. He had entered the room quietly, pausing long enough to see the injuries on Henry Lee's body. 'Now seems to be a good time to make good on it.'

From the door, Richard Hunt, his arm heavily bandaged and in a sling held tight against his chest, said, 'Don't leave me out. I want to help as well.'

# 11

## The Lily Wanderer — Mora Bay

'You seem restless,' Tung said.

'I have reason to be,' Traeger said. 'I wasn't expecting things to get so out of hand. This should have been running a lot easier. We have bodies left around the city. Too many bodies for my liking.'

'I never would have expected you to be so squeamish, Traeger.'

'The dead don't bother me. It's just how they attract attention from the law.'

'The police will blunder around for a while, as they always do. By the time they reach a decision, we will have moved our plans forward and accomplished what we set out to do.'

'You make it sound so damned easy.'

'Any path taken will have stumbling blocks. It's a case of anticipating and circumventing them.'

Traeger turned from the *The Lily Wanderer*'s cabin window and glanced across at the seated Tong Master. He could smell the slightly sweet smell of the smoke from the small clay pipe Tung held. Opium.

The Tong Master partook of the product he sold so willingly, though not in great amounts that would make him a slave to it like the unfortunates he bound to the drug. He used it as an occasional calming influence, and Traeger believed it was what kept the man in control of his actions. Tung was clever enough never to allow himself to be dominated to the drug. Many of the Chinese under his command used it to a greater degree, and Tung fed it to them as a reward for their loyalty.

Traeger had only tried it once, and it had sickened him so badly he refused to even think about using it again. He decide he would stick to a glass of whiskey if he needed to calm his nerves. He could have done with some right now. Even though *The Lily Wanderer* was at anchor in the relatively calm waters of the enclosed bay, the gentle movement of the vessel affected him. His stomach felt unsettled.

'When can we get off this damned boat?'

Tung managed a condescending smile as he leaned forward. 'Of course, you are not a lover of sailing, Traeger. To be honest, with all that's going on, I'd forgotten.'

'I hadn't . . . '

A hard fist rapped on the cabin door. Tung gave a command in Chinese and the door opened. It was Lo Keye. In English Tung asked, 'What is it?'

'The woman. She tried to break free.'

'Is she hurt?'

'We had to restrain her. She struck the guard bringing her food and tried to run. In the struggle to restrain her, she took a blow to her head.'

Tung stood. 'Is she conscious?'

Keye nodded. 'More angry than hurt.'

'The woman has spirit. Let's go and see her.'

They made their way to the fore-cabin, where Jasmine Soong was being held. She was seated on the bunk, closely watched by two of Tung's men.

'Now I'm being visited by the great man himself,' she said. 'Is this what it takes to get your attention, Tung?'

There was a red mark down the side of her face that must have been painful, yet there was no trace of fear in her voice as she got to her feet to confront Tung. Traeger stood to one side, a faint smile on his face.

'I see you have your eager puppy dog at your side, Tung.'

'I'm disappointed you feel you want to leave us,' Tung said. 'Is the accommodation not to your taste?'

'The surroundings could be worse, Tung. It's the foul stench in the air that offends me.'

'Someone in your position,' Traeger said, 'should be careful what you say.'

'Or what? You'll kill me? Wouldn't that rather be a waste of all the effort you've put into kidnapping me?'

'The young woman has a point, Traeger,' Tung said, a thin smirk on his lips. 'After all, we took Miss Soong so we could use her as a bargaining object. If she were dead, her father would no longer be persuaded to assist us.'

'Just why am I here, Tung? What do you want from my father?' Jasmine asked. 'No one's told me why I was taken.'

'All in good time,' Tung said. 'Right now I have a more pressing matter to attend to. I believe it may suggest to you that I'm serious in my intentions. Bring her.'

Tung led the way back on deck, where Chinese crewmembers were gathered. He began to address them in Chinese. A figure was pushed into view. He stood, head down.

'This is the man who failed to restrain you,' Tung said to Jasmine. 'His mistake could have allowed you to escape.'

Tung gestured to Keye. He moved quickly and confronted the lone Chinese. He struck with unrestrained brutality, his blows rendering the unfortunate man to the deck. A final palm-edged blow snapped the man's neck. He fell face down on the deck, body in spasm until death took him.

Jasmine turned away, a horrified gasp escaping her lips.

'Remember this if thoughts of escape fill your mind again,' Tung said. 'There may come a time when your presence may become more of a burden than your usefulness.'

Traeger eased the Tong leader aside. 'Tung, we need to get back to town. There are matters to attend to if Soong sends a message. The woman is secure. We can't afford to waste time here.'

'I suppose you're right,' Tung agreed. He faced his crew and gave orders in Chinese. Jasmine was escorted back to her cabin.

'You think your orders will be followed this time?' Traeger asked.

Tung allowed one of his rare smiles. 'They understand what will happen if any more mistakes occur.'

A small boat was moored at the side of *The Lily Wanderer*. It took Tung, Traeger and Lo Keye back to shore. A number of the hired guns were there, and Tung gave them their orders. They were to stay in the area in case anyone showed up.

Taking the reins of the buggy, Keye turned it around as Tung and Traeger settled in the seats, and they headed back in the direction of San Francisco.

# 12

Kilpatrick wore a pair of Cavalry-style Butternut pants held up by broad suspenders over a gray shirt. A much-used cloth coat covered the holstered revolver strapped around his waist, and a battered Derby hat was jammed on his head.

'Sergeant, just the sight of you'll make even a Tong man run away,' Hallows said, barely managing to keep a straight face.

'If that's the case, sir,' Kilpatrick said, 'then I'll be a happy man.' He reached under the back of his coat to show the lethal-looking wooden billy club he carried. 'Just in case I run out of bullets, you understand,' he added.

They had gathered in Hallows's office for a final discussion. Richard Hunt was there too, disappointment showing on his face at not being fit enough to join them. He had accepted the group decision, and in truth he understood. He was still weak from his wound and in no state to go riding across country on the back of a jogging horse. The doctor, too, was concerned and wanted to keep an eye on him.

'No strenuous maneuvers. That arm needs time for the damage to knit together. And you'll still be weak from blood loss for a while.'

'Fine. You're the doctor,' Hunt said. 'I just wanted to make my mark. The Chinese Tong is why I came to America in the first place.'

'From what I've heard,' Bodie said, 'you've already made your mark.'

'Still leaves me out of the main action.'

'Richard,' Brand said, 'staying at Doc Boyd's and watching over him is important. The Tong might have it on their minds to make a visit if they believe Henry Lee is still alive.'

'True enough,' Hallows said. 'They don't give up easily, and they're strong on retribution.'

'All right, Jason. I'm convinced. I'll get over there now,' Hunt said. He had his revolver holstered on his right hip, butt forward so he could easily reach it with his left hand. 'Good luck, chaps,' he said as he left.

Boyd wished them luck and followed Hunt out.

'The place Lee described,' Brand said. 'Where they might have Jasmine Soong . . . '

'About five miles outside the city,' Hallows said, indicating it on a map tacked to his office wall. 'The Belker place has been deserted for a few years since the original owner went bankrupt and left. Mora bay is here. No more than a couple of miles west.'

'I can find it,' Kilpatrick said. 'Give me a half hour and I'll have horses ready.'

After the Irishman had left, Brand and Bodie readied the weapons at hand. Hallows had provided long guns and ammunition for them.

'We could find ourselves facing a

strong force,' he pointed out.

'Then let's make sure we're loaded for bear,' Bodie said, a cold grin on his face. 'For a lot of damn bears. I'm in the mood for a hunt.'

'Is he always so cheerful?' Hallows asked.

'Bodie? Yeah, he always sees the funny side of any situation.'

'Nobody ever said that about me before.'

'Take it as a compliment.'

* * *

Kilpatrick showed up with four saddled horses. Mounted, they rode slowly through the busy streets until the city fell behind them and they picked up a well-beaten trail leading west. The ocean lay on their left, gradually slipping from sight as Kilpatrick veered slightly north. At first they found themselves riding by ranches and farms, the countryside lush and scattered with timber. The further they rode from San Francisco, the wider spread were the outfits.

Drawing rein in a scatter of trees, Kilpatrick thrust out an arm. 'There she is,' he said.

Beyond the trees, the terrain fell away in a long, sweeping view into a wide basin, bounded on all sides by open slopes. There was a generous house constructed in the Spanish style, with white walls and a deep red tiled roof; a number of strongly built corrals, an outhouse, and a pair of large barns. A wide stream, water sparkling in the sun, curved along the land. A tall windmill swung lazily in the slight breeze. The place had a deserted look to it, grass and undergrowth long and unattended.

'Now that,' Hallows said, 'is real pretty. Kind of place a man could take to and settle down.'

'Yeah?' Bodie said. 'So tell me why there isn't a moving soul, man or beast, in sight. Tell me that. Hell, maybe Tung has moved his people away.'

Even though they sat and studied the

layout for a good ten minutes, they saw nothing.

'If we circle around, we can come in back of the barns,' Brand suggested. 'Take a closer look.'

'I guess,' Hallows said. 'Since we rode all this way, be a shame not to.'

They stayed within the cover of the trees and made the long, slow ride around the rim of the basin until they were looking down on the far side of the spread. They dismounted and tied the horses under cover. Rifles in hand, they walked the slope that took them to the flatland and the back yard of the house, coming up to the solid bulk of the barns.

It was here they made a discovery. Moving down the side of the closest barn, they picked up muffled sounds coming from inside.

'If that ain't horses . . . ' Bodie said.

A side door allowed them access. The mingled odors of hay and feed, leather and horses met them. Down one wall were a number of stalls, and unsaddled horses stirred restlessly when they moved toward the main doors.

Brand paused to inspect a line of tracks in the hard packed-dirt floor. Marks left by iron-rimmed wheels. Some kind of buggy pulled by a two-horse team. He followed the tracks to the main door, where he crouched and checked the marks. Moisture was still seeping into the earth. He gestured to Bodie, and the manhunter made his own inspection.

'Few hours, I'd say. Somebody left.'

The tracks led to the main door, and when they eased one of the high doors open a few inches, they were able to see the buggy tracks lead off across the yard and out onto open land.

'If they left someone in the house,' Kilpatrick said, 'it's likely they'll know where the buggy went.'

# 13

Brand and Bodie took the frontal approach, leaving Inspector Hallows and Kilpatrick to cover the rear of the house. Giving the inspector and his sergeant time to get into position, Brand led his partner to the stoop, up the steps and paused at the front door. They stood on either side, weapons at the ready.

'Set?' Bodie asked.

Brand nodded and Bodie raised a booted foot, slamming it against the door. The lock shattered and the door flew wide. Bodie ducked inside, Brand on his heels. Almost immediately, there was a crash from the rear of the house. Voices were raised. A gun fired.

An armed man stepped from a door along the hallway. The moment he saw Brand and Bodie, he swept up the pistol he carried. He fired hastily, the slug tearing a strip of wood from the doorframe behind them.

Bodie and Brand fired together, and the shooter was twisted aside as .45 slugs slammed into his upper body. He slumped to the floor, a second man stepping over him, a pistol in each hand. Heavy .45 caliber slugs burned through the air. He was cursing loudly as he fired, his words lost in the hammer of gunfire, creating noise but little else.

Brand and Bodie flattened to the wall, avoiding the volley. Brand returned fire, remaining calm as he pushed his Colt forward, held for a few seconds before he fired. His slug struck the man above his left eye, sending him stumbling back.

⋆　⋆　⋆

Kilpatrick pushed his way through the back door. It led directly into the kitchen, where one man was tending to the cooking and a second was seated at a rough table, bent over a plate of food. The sudden appearance of the big Irishman caught the men off guard as they turned, startled.

Just then, gunfire erupted from the front of the house. 'Sonofabitch,' the seated man yelled. He went for the pistol holstered on his hip, kicking away his ladder-back chair and sending it across the floor.

Hallows, crowding behind Kilpatrick, witnessed the man's move. He raised his pistol and fired without a moment's hesitation. His slug thumped into the man's chest and sent him sprawling across the table.

The man at the stove was faster, drawing his holstered pistol in a smooth movement. He angled it in Kilpatrick's direction and triggered a single shot that tore hard across the Irishman's side. Kilpatrick returned fire even as he felt the impact, his well-placed shot striking the other in the chest. The man fell back against the stove, scattering cooking utensils as he fell, then dropped to the floor.

'Seamus,' Hallows said as the Irishman sagged against the door frame.

Kilpatrick clamped a big hand to his side, blood surging through his fingers. 'Nothing, sir,' he said. 'A scratch is all.'

'Scratch be damned, you stubborn man. Go sit down over there and stay while I go and see how Brand and Bodie are. That's an order, Sergeant.'

Hallows put away his pistol and checked his rifle before making for the door leading into the main house where he could hear additional shots.

★  ★  ★

There were two more armed men in the room that had housed the pair Brand and Bodie had faced.

Coolidge and Butler, a pair of gunmen employed by Traeger. It hadn't been difficult to find and hire them. Tung had advised Traeger where to locate them on the Barbary Coast section of the city. The job had been easy as far as the pair were concerned.

140

All they had been expected to do was be around and await orders from Traeger. If truth were told, it turned out to be fairly low-key. Not that Coolidge and Butler were too concerned about that. They were being paid, so there was no need to complain. It was easy pay. Lounging around in the house. Food and drink provided, even if the drink was only coffee. Hard liquor would have to wait until they returned to San Francisco.

The same had gone for Trego and Sims, the other pair who made up the bunch. Only, that situation had changed all of a sudden. Gunfire filled the house with its noise. Trego and Sims had responded to the sound of the front door being kicked open. They had rushed from the main room, guns up, and had walked into hostile fire. Their bloody bodies were in view outside the door, and though Coolidge and Butler reacted swiftly, they were not swift enough. A pair of armed figures rushed the doorway, guns up and sweeping the room.

Butler got off a single shot before return fire came, and Butler's left shoulder blossomed red as he took a slug that broke bone and tore out a chunk of flesh and muscle as it exited. Butler was jerked back by the force of the slug. He expelled a pained grunt as he dropped, letting go of his pistol.

The moment he fired, Brand went into a low crouch, allowing Bodie a clear field. The manhunter tracked his target and triggered two fast shots that hammered at Coolidge's chest. The impact stopped Coolidge in his tracks. He fell against the wall, sliding down to the floor, leaving a bloody smear behind.

Brand picked up a scuffling sound, turned, and saw Butler sliding himself across the floor until he was able to pull himself into a corner of the room. His right hand gripped his bloody shoulder and a low moan came from his lips. Brand spotted the gun the man had dropped and scooped it up, then turned as Butler let out a pained cry. Hunched against the angle of the walls, the man was hugging his damaged shoulder, eyes staring at Brand in a silent plea for help. Blood was pulsing from the wound, staining his hand and spilling down his shirt.

'Help . . . me . . . '

Brand crossed the room to stand over the injured man. 'Where's Tung? Traeger? And Jasmine Soong? Where've they gone?'

'Son of a bitch . . . '

'You got that part right. Now tell me what I want to know.'

'My shoulder . . . '

'Longer you hold out, the more it's going to hurt. Answer my question.'

'You got no damn right.'

'Nobody said anything about right.' Brand's voice rose to a shout. 'Answer my damn question.' He raised his foot and pressed the sole of his boot against Butler's bloody shoulder, applying pressure. Butler screamed. He stared up at Brand's taut face, and even in his agony he realized things would get worse if he didn't speak.

'Jasmine Soong?'

'She's on *The Lily Wanderer*. A coastal ship is all. It's moored in a small bay nearby. Mora Bay. They took her there. They'll keep her on board while they sail up and down the coast.'

It was, Brand decided, a smart move, keeping Jasmine Soong out of reach while Tung negotiated his terms with her father.

'How far?' Bodie asked.

'Couple of miles. Straight south from here. Can't miss it.'

'How many on board?'

'Tung has a crew.'

'When will they be leaving?'

'Not 'til dawn, from what I heard Tung telling Traeger.'

Brand removed his foot and stepped back. Clutching at his shoulder, Butler curled up, deep sobs escaping his lips. Feeling beads of sweat on his brow, Brand wiped it away with his sleeve.

'You might have killed me . . . ' Butler moaned. 'You miserable bastard.'

'I wouldn't go that far,' Bodie said

from behind Brand. 'At least not the miserable part.' He was standing in the doorway, gun hand at his side.

'They have Jasmine Soong.'

'Yeah, I heard,' Bodie said.

'You saw what he did,' Butler grumbled. 'You can tell the law.'

'All I heard was you shouting your mouth off. Didn't see a thing.'

'Damn liar.'

'Keep that up and I might give you a matching right shoulder,' Bodie said evenly.

'What about Tung and Traeger?' Brand said.

Butler had realized giving these men what they wanted was his best option. 'They headed back to the city a while back. It's the truth. We were supposed to stay around here in case . . . '

Bodie managed a cold smile. 'In case we showed up. Feller, they ain't going to be too pleased way you boys held up your end.'

★ ★ ★

They patched up Butler and Kilpatrick as best they could. It was crude bandaging that wasn't going to last for long.

'Get them back to San Francisco. They both need doctoring,' Bodie said. He stood checking his weapons; and Brand, watching him closely, knew what the manhunter was planning.

'It's going to be dark in a while,' he said.

'That's what I'm counting on,' Bodie said. 'And the hope that ship won't move out of that bay until dawn. Leaves me enough time.'

'For what, man?' Hallows asked.

'To get on board.'

'That's just foolishness. We can't just ride out and leave you,' Hallows protested. 'Tell him, Brand.'

'His choice.'

He understood Bodie's need to find Jasmine Soong and to do it on his own terms. And he knew there was no point arguing with the manhunter.

'Butler needs a doctor,' Bodie said.

'As fast as possible. If you don't get him back to town, he could die on you, and right now he's the only witness you have, Hallows. He's working for Traeger and Tung. He'll know things. He's your prisoner. You need his evidence. And Kilpatrick's hurt too.'

'I'll be fine,' Kilpatrick said.

'No, you're bleeding all over the place,' Bodie said. 'That wound is going to hold you back, and that means you'll hold us back. The condition you're in means you're a liability.'

Kilpatrick's eyes flashed with anger, and he would have lunged at Bodie if he hadn't been as weak as he was. Then he managed a grin. 'Damned if you're not bloody right.' He gestured to Hallows. 'Inspector, we should do what the man says.'

'What about you?' Hallows asked Brand.

Bodie interrupted, 'He came looking for Traeger. He's found him. He needs to break up that pair — Traeger and Tung. It's why he came to San Francisco.'

The silence hung over them until

Brand said, 'Watch these two. I'll get the horses ready. We need to head out straightaway.'

★   ★   ★

Darkness was fast approaching by the time they were ready to move out. As weak as he was, Kilpatrick sat his saddle in determined silence. Butler, his arm bound tight against his body to ease his shattered shoulder, had to be tied to his saddle. He was semiconscious by this time, but appeared to be hanging on to life.

'I'll bring her back,' Bodie said.

Brand, in his saddle, nodded. 'If anyone can . . .'

'Line me up a beer. I'm going to be a thirsty man when this is over.'

'I don't suppose they'll be of a mind to give Miss Soong up without a fight,' Hallows said.

Bodie's grin had a predatory wolf's intensity to it. 'Hell, I hope not. I'm counting on it.'

'Bodie,' Brand said, 'that's what I like about you. All heart and brotherly love.'

'Don't you go spreading that rumor around. Won't do my reputation any favors.'

'Boyo, give 'em hell,' Kilpatrick said as he led off.

# 14

*Of all the crazy things I ever did, this
has to be at the top of the list.*

Bodie didn't question why he was
doing it. He already knew the answer:
because he had agreed to do it. And
whatever bad traits he might have pos-
sessed, going back on his word was not
one of them.

*So you can't blame a damn soul 'cept
yourself.*

Even with that said, it failed to it
make him feel any better.

He took his horse and tethered it in
the stable, then took his blanket roll
and canteen. He left his Winchester, but
kept his handgun and the sheathed knife,
and left the silent house behind as he
walked south, heading in the direction
of the coast and the bay Butler had told
about.

*Bodie, you're going to look like one*

150

*damn fool if that ship has sailed.*

He set a steady pace, easing through the brush and timber. The darkness was eased by a good moon that laid a pale light over the way. Bodie didn't rush. If Butler's information was correct, he had until daylight at least.

★   ★   ★

The bay lay calm and smooth, gleaming under the moonlight. The water broke gently against the sandy beach that extended some twenty feet up to the treeline, where Bodie crouched in shadow and studied the vessel moored some thirty feet from shore.

As *The Lily Wanderer* was a coastal ship, it had a reduced profile with a shallow draft and stood low in the water. Bodie saw lamps lit, strung along the deck. More lamplight shone through the windows of the cabin structure.

Bodie wrapped his blankets around his shoulders and leaned back against a tree. He would wait until it started to get light. That was the best time to make his move — while the crew was still resting; the early hours when a man's responses were at their slowest.

He lowered his eyes, his mind going over the events that had taken place since his arrival in San Francisco. He had located Jasmine Soong, but at a cost. Henry Lee was dead. So was Li Hung. Two more to add to his conscience, dead because they had been helping him. He wouldn't forget that. Kwai Fu Tung had plenty to answer for.

Bodie gripped the butt of his Colt, slid the pistol clear of the holster, and felt the cold steel of the weapon. That would change when he started to use it. Then it would grow hot, warmed by the slugs that would course along the barrel when he faced Tung's soldiers and took Jasmine Soong from them.

He sat out the long hours with the patience born of his trade. Waiting was part of his business. In the heat of the desert. The chill of a mountain slope. Watching . . . waiting . . . patient as he let his quarry come to him.

Bodie. The Stalker.

★ ★ ★

He saw the early dawn; let the light creep in and drive away the deep shadows. Then he slipped off his coat and hat and pushed them out of sight in the foliage along with his gun rig, keeping his Colt. He moved before full light, moving along the shore until he was a distance from the ship. Then he eased into the water, feeling the chill soak through his clothing.

Bodie was no great swimmer, but he knew enough to keep himself afloat, the Colt in his right hand held clear of the water. He judged there was about sixty feet between him and *The Lily Wanderer*. Distance enough. It was helpful that the bay calmed the waters, with little in the way of surges. He kept the ship on his right, coming up at the stern. More than once, he paused to check the deck. He spotted movement halfway along the length as a crewman moved briefly. Apart from that, there was little activity.

He was breathing hard by the time he reached the stern. There he pressed against the hull, then reached up and grasped the rail edging the deck. Pulling himself up out of the water, he peered through the rails and took a long, slow look across the deck. The single sail was furled. The open aspect of the deck showed the raised covers of the hold, and lamplight showed through the windows further along the outline of the cabin structure.

Bodie checked for any signs of movement on deck. With Jasmine Soong as a hostage, the Tong Master needed to keep her secure and out of sight, so there would no doubt be some form of protection. It would have helped to know just how many people were on board. A single young woman wouldn't need an army to keep her subdued. At least, Bodie hoped not.

He continued to peer into the gloom

and was rewarded as a lone figure came into sight: a single man, Chinese, clad in black, cradling a rifle in his arms. Bodie watched him move towards the stern, and lowered himself until only his eyes were visible along the base of the rail. The sentry paced to within a few feet, and Bodie saw he was looking out across the bay, his eyes focused on the shoreline as the light of early dawn extended itself. Nothing caught his attention, and he turned about and looked along the length of the deck. Bodie picked up the low murmur of the man's voice as he talked to himself. Then he started moving again, away from Bodie. He didn't appear to be in any kind of hurry, stopping every now and again, head turning left and right.

Bodie pulled himself up the stern, reaching for the top of the rail. He secured a hold with his feet, hauled himself over, and landed on the deck. He knew he had to make his next move quickly and without hesitation. If the Chinese realized he was there, the rifle he carried was going to make one hell of a difference. And Bodie's knife needed to be up close before it could be effective.

He tucked the Colt behind his belt and drew his knife from its sheath, gripping the handle, and stepped away from the rail. As quiet as he was, however, his movement and the drip of water from his clothes reached the keen ears of the sentry. He turned, taking in the tall, drenched American, and swung the rifle from rest into his hands.

Bodie launched himself forward, his attempt at caution forgotten. His right arm extended, the heavy-bladed knife snapped forward to reach and impale itself in the man's throat. With all of Bodie's strength behind it, the blade slid in up to the hilt. The sentry had no chance to call out as the razor-sharp blade cut through everything in its path. As he stumbled back, Bodie let go of the knife and snatched the rifle from his hands. He saw it was a new .44-40 Winchester and worked the lever, watching a shiny cartridge spring from the port. The sentry had dropped to the deck, his limbs jerking as he struggled for breath that was never going to come. As Bodie stepped over the man, crouching, he grasped the knife and pulled it free, sliding it back into the sheath on his belt.

A shrill cry alerted him and, still bent over the dying man, he saw a dark-clad figure erupt from behind the cabin housing, clawing at a revolver pushed behind the wide cloth sash around his waist. The Winchester arced up. In Bodie's capable hands, it tracked the moving man and hammered out a shot, the slug finding its target in the man's chest. He hit the deck rail at his side and toppled over.

As Bodie levered a fresh round into the breech, he heard a door crash as it was flung open. He dropped to his knees behind the first cargo hatch cover he reached, seeing a couple more black-clad men appear. They were shouting orders to each other as they spilled out onto the deck. Both were armed with rifles similar to the one Bodie had gotten his hands on. He shouldered the Winchester, aimed and fired, catching the first man in the shoulder, who reeled from the impact and the sudden pain. Bodie re-aimed and put a second slug into him, aware that a wounded adversary could still have the strength and purpose to fight on. His second .44-40 slammed between the target's eyes and he toppled backwards.

The sound of a shot came from the second man, who managed to blow a chunk of wood from the lip of the hatch cover inches from Bodie. He felt the sting of splinters as he ducked, scooting to the far side of the hatch before rising on one knee and catching the man, who cleared the end of the cabin structure, the muzzle of his rifle searching for the American. Bodie put three fast shots into his chest, flinging him back and dropping him down, the rifle slipping from dead hands and sliding across the deck.

Knowing how matters could change quickly, Bodie broke cover and reached the shelter of the cabin housing, flattening against the comer. He could hear rapid speech as additional reinforcements made their move. He slid into a low crouch, leaned around the comer of the cabin, and met the rush of figures head on. The men came at him accompanied by a chorus of screams and yells, a number of them brandishing swords and knives. Bodie concentrated on the ones carrying guns as he fired and levered, repeating the action over and over, sending a heavy volley at the men scrambling along the deck. His slugs found their targets, who suddenly found their mass attack had done little apart from making them the unwilling victims of Bodie's concentrated strike. They were facing a man who had dealt with strong odds before; and if there was one thing Bodie had learned, it was to hold his nerve and not back down.

The rush broke, the men stepping back, giving Bodie the opportunity to reach and pick up a discarded rifle. He threw aside the one he'd been using and brought his new weapon into play, scattering the remaining men with well-placed shots that hammered them to the deck. Gunsmoke drifted away as Bodie moved forward, stepping past the bodies. He saw a fallen pistol and scooped it up to tuck in his belt, then peered through the windows he passed. The interior of the main cabin appeared empty, but he moved on with caution uppermost in his mind. It didn't do to accept a situation on first glance. When he reached the door the men had emerged from, he edged it wide with his foot, the muzzle of the Winchester probing ahead. The inside of the cabin was empty, with a door at the end leading further into the ship. He figured there would be crew cabins ahead.

At the door, Bodie leaned the rifle against the bulkhead and took out the pistol he'd picked up, leaving his own Colt in place. His acquired weapon was a long-barreled Colt Peacemaker. He dropped down, firing at a moving shape along the companionway, and was rewarded by a stunned grunt. The shape came forward, hit but still able to move. Bodie raised the Colt and triggered a second shot. The man straightened up, throwing his arms wide as he took the slug, then tumbled as his legs gave way. Moving forward, Bodie bent and picked up the revolver the man had dropped. Now he had a third handgun.

A woman's voice cried out from behind the door of one of the cabins. Bodie picked up the sound of a struggle. Someone slammed against the cabin door. The upper wood panel split and the door swung wide, a slim black-haired young Chinese woman stumbling out. Jasmine Soong.

'Stay down,' Bodie yelled; and she flattened to the deck.

Bodie had seen an armed man behind her wielding a long-barreled shotgun. The man saw Bodie. He brought the barrel of the shotgun round. The weapon hit the doorframe, and the man pulled it back to readjust his aim.

Bodie raised both pistols and fired a number of shots that hit the man in the chest. He staggered back across the cabin, then crashed to the deck in a squirming sprawl.

'Any others in there?' Bodie asked.

Jasmine Soong brushed hair back from her face, giving Bodie a long stare. 'No,' she said.

'Good. Now let's get out of here.' Bodie pushed one of the revolvers behind his belt and reached down to help her to her feet.

'Tell me something, Mister . . . ?'

'Bodie.'

'Do you do this kind of thing often?'

'Has been known, Miss Soong.'

He led the way to the deck, skirting the men stretched out across the deck, Jasmine staying close behind him. He heard her gasp when she saw the bodies.

'I can see, Mr. Bodie, that you weren't far from telling the truth.'

Bodie scanned the open deck, his pistol cocked and raised. Nothing. He could hear the water lapping against the side of the ship, and the creak of the mast and rigging.

'Are we waiting for something?' Jasmine asked. Then she added, 'And how do you know my name? I don't know who you are.'

'Ruby Keoh asked me to help. Lawyer Bainbridge had a hand in it too. And I'm sure your father's in there somewhere.'

'You know Ruby?'

'Yes, ma'am.'

Her hand touched his sleeve. 'I'm forgetting my manners, Mr. Bodie. Thank you for rescuing me from these terrible people.'

'Thank me later. We need to get away from here. I have a feeling Tung isn't going to be a happy man when he finds out what's happened.'

'You believe he might . . . '

The question remained unanswered as a slug thudded into the deck rail a foot away from where they were standing. Splinters flew into the air. Bodie grabbed Jasmine's arm, dragging her the length of the cabin and around the far end, where they at least had some cover. Their assailants were on the not-too-distant shoreline, Bodie guessed from the trajectory of the slug. More of Tung's hired guns. Butler had said there might be more of them in the area. He watched armed figures slide a small rowboat from cover in the foliage and drag it to the water. They launched it and began to move it towards *The Lily Wanderer*.

Bodie and Jasmine hunkered down, and Bodie checked his weapons. Three loads in one, two in the other. He transferred the loads to one pistol and threw the empty one over the side. He still had his own weapon holding six loads. He could feel Jasmine's fingers clutching at his sleeve.

'What do we do now? I don't suppose you know how to sail a boat?' she said.

'No. But I know how to make one burn.'

# 15

Bodie had seen lamps suspended over the deck, still lit from the previous night. He reached up and took a couple.

'What are you going to do?' Jasmine asked.

'Try to gain us some cover.' He raised the wicks as far as they would go, unscrewed the filler caps, and swung the lamps against the cabin structure. Oil spilled down the bleached wood and ignited. Then he repeated the action with a number of the other lamps. The dry timber burned, flame spreading and smoke starting to gather and rise. 'Let's move around the other side,' he said.

Jasmine followed, and they slipped around the cabin. 'Mr. Bodie, are you trying to burn us to death?'

'Not hardly.'

As the cabin fire spread, more smoke billowed, fanned by the slight morning breeze. Where oil had spilled across the deck, the planking caught and the flames spread. Bodie led Jasmine to the stern of the ship. 'The water's fairly shallow, and we're close to the shore.'

She frowned at him. 'Are you expecting us to swim?'

'Can you walk on water, Miss Soong?'

'Of course not.'

'There we are then.' He slipped over the transom, holding the rail with one hand and offering his other to Jasmine.

'At least before you came I was able to keep my feet dry,' she said.

Despite her misgivings, she lowered herself into the water. Bodie slipped an arm around her waist and kept her close. He eased them around to the side of the ship away from the shore, and managed to keep their heads above water as he floated them the length of the vessel until they were at the bow, where he was able to see the approaching rowboat. Smoke was curling around from the burning deck, lifting and falling in the breeze. He could hear the men in the boat as they peered through the drifting smoke. They appeared to be having conflicting ideas about how they should proceed. As long as they were occupied with that, their attention might be distracted, Bodie thought. Whatever he did now was going to put himself and Jasmine at greater risk, but they had little choice.

The moment the rowboat began to slide along the length of the ship, Bodie moved himself and Jasmine away from the bow and struck out for the shoreline. 'Just kick your legs,' he said. 'I'll keep you above water.'

Jasmine did as he suggested, and they moved away from *The Lily Wanderer*. Behind them, the vessel was. well ablaze now. Flames were slowly engulfing the deck, creeping up the masts and rigging. Sparks made orange sprays as they were caught by the breeze and flung about. The smoke was thicker now, curling and eddying, rising over the stricken ship.

Bodie concentrated his efforts on getting them to the beach and the treeline that would at least offer them added protection. If they could reach it before the men in the boat realized they were no longer on board . . .

The shout came from behind them, followed by a wild shot that came close.

Bodie's feet touched bottom. He pushed forward, pulling Jasmine with him. As the water shallowed, they were both able to stand upright. 'We head for the trees,' he said. 'And don't stop.'

They stumbled ashore, Bodie grabbing Jasmine's hand and pulling her along beside him. He was not gentle, yet she made no protest as they made their way across the sand and into the cover of the trees and vegetation. Thin tendrils slapped at their bodies and caught at their faces. Bodie kept moving, with no particular destination in mind, simply gaining distance between them and Tung's men.

He came to a stop and gestured for

Jasmine to stay low. She did as she was told, panting as she caught her breath. She had the good sense not to speak as Bodie crouched next to her, scanning back the way they had come, ears straining to pick up any sound that might tell them how close their pursuers were. He heard distant noises: someone was pushing through the foliage and not being too quiet about it. Then more sounds from another point — someone working their way through the brush. The rowboat crew had reached shore and were moving in.

'Persistent, I'll give 'em that,' he whispered.

'My goodness, knowing that really helps, Mr. Bodie. I'm feeling so much better now.' Jasmine had a couple of thin scratches on her face, and her clothes were still damp from the water, but she maintained her streak of sassiness.

Someone was drawing closer. Bodie saw the foliage shiver as the dark bulk of a man stepped into an open patch. He was hard-looking, long hair spilling over the collar of his checked shirt, a pistol in his left hand. His head was casting back and forth as he moved forward, his gaze dropping to the ground, searching. He must have picked up their tracks, as he straightened up and moved in a direct line to where Bodie and Jasmine were concealed.

Bodie considered his move. He knew the man was not alone. How many comrades did he have?

Further concern was put on hold as the Tong moved closer still. Bodie had to do something, fast. And he needed to keep any confrontation as silent as possible.

He let the pistol fall from his hand and slid his knife from the sheath on his hip. Then he passed the keen-bladed weapon to his left hand, leaving his right free to deal with the oncoming gunman. The man was almost at the brush concealing Bodie and Jasmine.

It was as far as he got.

Bodie stepped forward, grabbed the man's gun hand, and yanked him forward and onto the blade of the knife he was wielding. A shocked expression crossed the man's face as he felt the cold steel slide into his body. Bodie pushed it in as far as it could go, then removed the pistol from the man's hand with a vicious yank. As the man folded up, Bodie pulled the knife free and jammed it back into its sheath.

Behind him, Jasmine made a choking sound, hands raised to her shocked white face. Bodie checked the pistol and saw it had six filled chambers. He left the water-soaked gun on the ground.

'Jasmine, let's move. He wasn't on his own. His friends must be around here somewhere.'

'You . . . '

'Yeah, I killed him. He wasn't looking to invite us for tea and sympathy. And neither will his partners.' Bodie caught her arm, hard. 'You want to go back to Tung? To whatever he has waiting for you?' She shook her head. 'Then let's move. Now.'

He propelled her through the brush, knowing that any time he might had gained for them was slipping away. Tung's hired guns would soon realize one of their number was out of the game, so they needed to stay ahead of any pursuit.

# 16

Bodie heard the heavy sound of horses being pushed through the brush. The men from the boat must have had them close by. That changed the rules. He was ill-equipped to deal with mounted opposition, his own animal being stabled at the house a distance away and in the opposite direction to the one he and Jasmine were going. It just added to the problems he already had. Not that he was about to give up. The thought never crossed his mind.

'Time we moved,' he said.

'How can . . . '

She didn't get the chance to complete her question. Behind them and coming closer, Bodie could hear the bulk of the horses as the riders closed the gap. As if she had suddenly grasped the severity of their situation, Jasmine put on a spurt, long legs carrying her ahead of Bodie. Despite her agility, however, there was no way she could outrun a horse.

Bodie caught a fleeting glimpse of a horse and rider emerging from the greenery. The rider was urging his mount on, the animal eating up the distance, its head stretched out, mane flying back over its neck, hooves pounding the soft earth of the forest. A second rider was moving up, angling in Bodie's direction, clearly intending to separate them.

The rider chasing after Jasmine spurred his horse forward and passed Bodie. The rider leaned forward, arm reaching out to catch hold of Jasmine's dress as he leveled with her. Bodie heard her scream before she was lifted off her feet and pulled over the saddle. He sensed the bulk of the other horse moving alongside him and tried to move out of its path, but the heavy weight of the animal slammed into him, and his feet left the ground as he was sent flying.

He hit the ground and bounced and rolled, his senses jarred by the impact.

As soft as it was, the forest floor drove the breath from his body. Bodie threw out his left hand to brake his fall, taking most of it across the shoulders. His forward motion only ceased when he slammed against the base of a tree. He struggled to regain his balance, ignoring the dull ache that swept across his body. Bodie threw out a hand and pushed it against the trunk of the tree that had halted his forward movement. He understood enough to know that the rider who had put him down would be coming back. He twisted his head to look, and there the rider was, reining his horse around and slamming in his heels to urge the animal on.

'Sonofabitch,' Bodie muttered. 'Now you've done it.' He was furious; and whenever he reached that state of mind, he was not about to lie back and quit. He sucked in a breath, levered himself to one knee, and brought up the pistol still in his hand.

The oncoming rider saw the rising pistol and realized he had not accounted for the manhunter's resilience. There was no way he would be able to turn his horse aside, so he did the only thing he could. He dropped his hand to the holstered pistol on his side.

He was too slow and far too late.

Bodie put a pair of shots into him. One caught his throat and the second took him in the chest. The man rolled back in his saddle, lost his grip and went over the horse's rear end, trailing a spume of blood. He slammed to the ground face down, hard, but by then he was too far gone to notice.

Bodie lurched to his feet, eyes searching for the rider who had taken Jasmine. He caught a fragmented image of the rider weaving through the timber and raised his pistol before realizing there was no way he would get a clear shot in amongst the timber. He needed to be closer.

He turned about and, seeing that the riderless horse had come to a halt, pushed the pistol behind his belt and approached it slowly. The animal swung its head round and eyed him. Bodie reached out and took hold of the dangling reins, drew the horse close, and patted its neck. As he swung into the saddle, he was reminded of the hurt his body had undergone and knew he was going to be suffering. But right now that didn't matter. He turned the horse and set it after the rider who had Jasmine. Seeing that there was a saddle gun in the leather scabbard, he drew it out and checked it. It was a .44 caliber Henry. A well cared-for rifle. Sixteen shots in the magazine if it was fully loaded.

He urged the horse forward. He needed to close the gap between himself and the rider who had Jasmine. That was his priority now.

# 17

Bodie could see Jasmine hanging limply across the saddle in front of the rider. As the horses broke from the trees, starting to cross an open stretch, he saw his chance. He hauled his mount to a dead stop, rising in his stirrups, and brought the Henry to his shoulder. Then he pulled down on the distant target, hoping the rifle shot true, held his target and touched the trigger. He felt the Henry jerk back against his shoulder as it fired.

The .44 caliber slug struck just below the rider's hat brim. It jerked the man forward and he pitched over, slipping sideways off the horse's back. His right foot caught in the stirrup and he hung limply. The unaccustomed weight made the horse slow and stop.

Bodie drew rein alongside, easing his bruised body from the saddle. He reached up and slid Jasmine from the horse, holding her slim form in his arms as he moved her away. He could feel her stirring sluggishly and saw the bruise across her right cheek where the rider had struck her. He laid her on the ground, went back to the horse and took the canteen he saw. Then he returned and knelt beside her, uncapping the canteen and splashing dribbles of water over her face until she opened her eyes, staring up at him. Panic gripped her before she recognized him.

'This is becoming a habit, Mr. Bodie. You rescuing me from bad men.'

'Let's hope this is the last time.'

Jasmine's gaze was drawn to the sprawled body. She failed to repress a shudder when she saw what Bodie's shot had done. 'Because of that man, Tung, there seems to have been a great deal of violence and dying.'

Bodie inspected the bruise of her face. 'You seem to be having your share of hard treatment. As for Tung, his time is coming, believe me.' He helped

Jasmine to her feet. 'Can you ride?'

'If it helps us to get away from all this, I'll ride, Mr. Bodie.'

# 18

Dr. Boyd stood on the boardwalk outside his office alongside Richard Hunt, mugs of coffee in their hands. They were watching as a tight bunch of riders came along the street; it was obvious they were heading for Boyd's place. It was still early morning, with few people about. If Boyd had been expecting a slow day, he was about to be disappointed.

'That's Brand,' Hunt said.

'Hallows and Kilpatrick,' Boyd said, recognizing the lawmen.

The four riders halted in front of them. 'The man called Butler has a bad shoulder and arm wound,' Hallows said. 'And Kilpatrick needs some attention too.'

'See to the man first,' Kilpatrick said.

Boyd handed his coffee mug to Hunt, then moved forward, assisting

Hallows and Brand in getting Butler off his horse. The man was barely awake, his wounded shoulder and arm a mass of congealed and darkened blood. He dragged his feet as he was maneuvered inside the doctor's office.

'Can I give you a hand, Sergeant?' Hunt said.

'And disturb your own wound? I'll be fine, Captain, but thank you for the offer.'

The Irishman slid from his saddle and stood for a moment. When Hunt offered him one of the coffee mugs, he took it gratefully, gulping the hot liquid quickly.

'You should get yourself inside and let the doctor look at you,' Hunt suggested.

'Yeah, go on and get yourself checked out Sergeant,' Brand said as he stepped back outside.

Kilpatrick nodded. 'I think that might be a good idea, sir. I must admit to feeling a mite weak.'

The Irishman went inside.

'A successful endeavor?' Hunt asked.

'We faced off Tung's hired guns. But Tung and Traeger gave us the slip and by now they should be back in the city.'

Hallows joined them.

'I should take a walk to my office,' he said, 'in case there are matters I need to attend to.'

'If anything happens, I'll let you know,' Brand said.

Hunt watched the inspector leave. 'I'm sure they will,' he said. 'Things happen.'

'They do, Richard, old chum.'

They were both right.

★　★　★

Butler let out a pained moan as Boyd peeled off the bloody bandage. The doctor made a cursory examination of the messy wound. Broken bone showed in the ragged flesh, and even with his scant view the doctor could see there was little he would be able to do for the damage. He glanced across at the patiently waiting Kilpatrick.

'Seamus, how are you doing?' he asked.

The Irishman shrugged. 'Next to that poor sod, I only have a scratch.'

'I need to deal with Butler right now.'

'Then do it. I'm not about to keel over and die on you.'

Boyd soaked a pad in chloroform and placed it over Butler's face, holding it there until he lapsed into unconsciousness. Then he pulled on a long white smock, washed his hands, and gathered his instruments. Before he saw to Butler, he checked Kilpatrick's side and cleaned it, wrapping a wide bandage around his body.

'You'll need stitches in that. I'll treat it further after I've done with Butler.'

'What are his chances?' Hunt asked.

'Chances? That he'll likely live but end up with a crippled arm. The bullet has ripped his bone to shreds and probably damaged nerves and muscle. All I can do is patch him up and hope he doesn't catch an infection.'

Brand had stepped back inside the doctor's office, leaving Hunt to stand outside for a minute. As he started to turn around to make his own way back inside himself, Hunt spotted a couple of Chinese on the opposite side of the street. They were making a show of looking in the window of a bootmaker, appearing to be interested in the display behind the glass. Something in their manner aroused Hunt's curiosity. When he turned about, he glanced into the widow of Boyd's office, where he could see the reflected images of the Chinese pair. Now that he had his back to them, they were staring at him.

Hunt pushed open the door of the doctor's office and stepped inside. As he closed the door, he stepped to the side. Staying in the cover of the inner window frame, he watched as the Chinese pair made their slow way across the busy street. They were moving directly towards the office. And from the staring expression on their faces, they weren't on a house call.

*Bloody hell*, the Englishman thought, *no walking away from this*. He slipped his Colt from its holster, easing back the hammer. 'Jason,' he called.

Brand came out of the back room and joined him at the door.

'Visitors,' Hunt said. 'And I don't see them as very friendly.'

As Brand looked on, the Chinese produced weapons from beneath their tunics. He pushed the door shut. 'Definitely not friendly.'

The two Chinese stepped up on the boardwalk, launching kicks at the door, sending it crashing back open. They came straight through into the office. Hunt had already backed off, raising his drawn pistol as the black-clad Chinese confronted him. The Englishman didn't hesitate, moving faster than the newcomers might have expected, taking the fight directly to them. The Colt thundered loudly in the confines of the office and the closest intruder, clutching a short-handled hatchet, spun away as the .45 caliber lead slug embedded itself in his chest.

As his companion dropped, the other Chinese launched himself in Hunt's direction, slashing the air with the wide long-bladed knife he was wielding. Hunt backed up, attempting to bring his Colt on target, but the frantic close-up attack forced him to lose the advantage. The Chinese made an angry howl, striking out again. The blade of his knife struck the barrel of the pistol, jarring it from Hunt's grasp. He took a hasty step back, heel catching against the edge of the carpet laid across the floor. He stumbled, falling, recognized the wild expression in the Chinese man's eyes, and realized — without it doing him any good — that the man was under the influence of opium. His drugged condition had pushed him into a state of violent excess.

'Hey!' Brand yelled.

The exclamation, delivered in a commanding tone, distracted the Chinese. He flicked his head around and found himself staring into the barrel of Brand's .45. Yet in his drugged condition he still went for Brand, who fired from no more than a couple of feet away. The Chinese went down heavily.

Hunt picked up his discarded pistol and climbed to his feet. 'I owe you for that, Jason,' he said.

'Can't abide people barging in like that.'

Hunt nodded. 'Something tells me we've upset Mr. Tung.'

Brand had bent over the Chinese, sniffing the air. 'These two smell heavily of opium. Giving themselves a boost.'

'What in the world's been going on here?' Dr. Boyd stood framed in the back-room doorway.

'A couple of Tung's thugs,' Hunt said.

'It appears to me that heathen is determined to make life difficult for us all,' Hunt said.

'It seems so,' the doctor agreed. 'What were they after?'

'At a guess, Henry Lee. Wanting to

finish what they started when he broke away from them.'

'Their information wasn't so good, then. They didn't even know the poor fellow's already dead.'

'Tung wants to make sure he removes anyone who could stand in his way,' Hunt said.

'How will he feel if Bodie succeeds in rescuing Jasmine Soong?'

'What if he fails?' Boyd said.

'Right now that's something I don't want to consider,' Brand said.

# 19

Bodie and Jasmine Soong showed up at the police station later that morning, having reclaimed his gear and horse before they had ridden away from the hideaway house. When Bodie asked for Hallows, the inspector took one look at him and quickly directed them through to his office.

'Are you hurt, Miss Soong?'

Jasmine shook her head. 'A little damp is all, Inspector.'

'How did you manage to get her away from Tung's people?' Hallows asked.

'We managed.'

'Mr. Bodie is being modest,' Jasmine said. 'He confronted my kidnappers and dealt with them. Then set fire to the boat to cause a distraction before we took horses. And here we are.'

'By confronted, you mean ... ' Hallows said.

'It involved a great deal of shooting,' the young woman said. 'Mostly by Mr. Bodie.'

Bodie said, 'Miss Soong is still a little shaken from what happened.'

'Please, don't make so little of it. If it hadn't been for his actions, things may not have ended so well for me.'

'Where's Brand?' Bodie asked. When Hallows told him, Bodie said he needed to join him. 'Hallows, I don't know what Tung might do if he finds out Jasmine's back in town. I need you to keep her here, protected.'

'You believe Tung might try to get to her again?'

'Let's plan for the worst.'

'She'll be safe here. There's a whole police station to look out for her,' Hallows said. 'What are you planning to do, Mr. Bodie?'

'I figured you'd know,' he said. 'It's time to end this. For good.'

# 20

In Boyd's office, Bodie stood and listened to what Brand had to say. The most important piece of information had come from Butler. The chloroform administered by the doctor during his work on the Butler's shoulder had loosened his tongue and he had been talking a great deal. Although there had been a deal of nonsense in his speech, he did confirm that the warehouse where Henry Lee had been taken was where Tung stored his large consignment of opium as well as other contraband.

'It'll make me a happy man to see that stuff taken away from Tung and Traeger,' Bodie said. 'Damnit, Jason, it's what this is all about. I don't see that hombre making a profit for all the misery it's caused.'

'Kind of matches my own feelings,' Brand said.

Bodie finished checking his Colt, jammed it back in the holster, and turned his attention to the Greener he had borrowed from the police station armory. He slid a pair of 12-gauge shells in place and locked the breech, dropping extra shells in his pocket, glancing across at Brand who had just checked his own weapons. 'You set for this?' he asked.

'Surprised you even have to ask,' Brand said.

'I've had my fill of San Francisco. Let's get this done so we can go home.'

They took a slow walk through the streets until they reached the waterfront area and located Tung's premises. In the cover of the last warehouse before Tung's, they viewed their target.

'Looks peaceful enough from here,' Bodie said.

'What we want is inside.'

They eased out of the shadows and stepped into the open. The Tung warehouse stood isolated, wide and seemingly deserted. No sound. No movement.

It was too peaceful.

They crossed the open jetty. On their left, the Pacific rolled against the dock pilings, lapping against the timbers. Gulls whirled and swooped out of the sky. A single figure leaned out from a partly open door, spotted the approaching pair, and quickly drew back out of sight.

'Had a feeling that might happen,' Brand said.

They broke into a run, closing the gap, and came up short against the bleached boards of the warehouse. The gaping door was pushed open and an armed man stepped into view, bringing up the rifle he carried. He was at an awkward angle, so the first shot went wide. Bodie fired the Greener from the waist, the burst scattering only briefly so that the man took a hefty charge. He was flung back, his body almost cut in half. In the empty moment, Bodie ran forward past the open door and flattened against the warehouse front on the opposite side. Voices were raised inside, a mix of Chinese and English.

Someone fired from inside, slugs clearing the open door, finding no targets. Bodie raised a hand, jerking it to indicate he was going to move around the warehouse. He moved fast, skirting the corner, and made his way along the side. He opened the shotgun, plucking out the used cartridge and replacing it with one from his pocket. There were no windows except those high up near the roofline, so he wasn't going to be spotted from inside. The downside was that any rear entrance could work as an exit. He found that out as he neared the back corner of the building. A Chinese man appeared, wielding a rifle, eyes scanning the side of the warehouse. His rifle swung up as he saw Bodie.

As Bodie took a shallow roll forward, he heard the weapon fire. The slug burned the air above him. The Chinese man uttered a sharp yell, running forward, and brought the rifle's muzzle down to line up on Bodie. Flat down on the ground, Bodie pushed the Greener in front of him, angling the muzzle forward and tripped both triggers. The shotgun jerked in recoil as twin lances of flame hit the Tong man in the upper chest and neck. Bodie saw him flung backwards in a flash of red, thumping to the ground on his back, legs kicking in dying spasms.

Bodie pushed to his feet, reloading again, and continued on towards the rear of the warehouse.

He picked up the sharp crackle of a Winchester from where he had left Brand.

★   ★   ★

Impatience overcoming caution, Brand lowered to a crouch and went in through the open door, breaking to the left as he made out a stack of filled bales, wooden kegs and crates. His move caught whoever was inside the warehouse. He had gained cover before shots hammered the silence. He heard slugs strike the cover he had found.

Whispered voices reached him, and the scrape of movement as someone changed position. Brand gauged at least three. There could have been more deeper in the warehouse.

He heard a distant shot from outside the building, then a double blast as a shotgun fired both barrels. Brand saw dark figures emerging from the scattered goods around the warehouse.

A rush of sound caught his ears. He turned and saw the glitter of a metal blade slashing the air as a fast-moving figure emerged from the shadows. A slashing blade cut down at him, and Brand turned sideways on, his rifle pushed forward to parry the downward blow. He felt the vibration as the Chinese sword came into contact with his Winchester, biting against the steel. The rifle was jarred from his grasp. He countered by snatching out the Colt holstered on his hip, dropping low and thrusting the .45 forward, hammer snapping back as he cocked the weapon. He caught a blurred glimpse of his attacker, the face twisted in an angry scowl as the man reversed the sword and made a second strike. The sword blade sliced Brand's sleeve, scoring his flesh. The Colt fired and the heavy lead slug burned its way into the Tong's throat. The man fell back, dropping his sword and clutching at his torn flesh.

As he slid between the stacked goods, Brand drew his second pistol from the shoulder holster and fired when he saw a moving figure. The man dropped without a sound. Brand had set himself now, his nerves steady, his aim steadier as he confronted his adversaries. He fired his pistols from both hands, eyes adjusted to the gloom; and he moved with a confident stride that pushed the opposition back, his shots hitting home with precision.

★   ★   ★

Bodie held the Greener chest-high as he hit the flimsy rear door on the move, weathered timber splintering under his assault. He ducked through the opening, breaking to the left, the shotgun leveling to a firing position. He caught hurried movement close by, heard the rattle of a shot, and felt the slug score his left cheek. Instinctively he dropped to one knee, the twin bores of the Greener cutting the air and settling on the scowling face of the shooter. Bodie's finger stroked the first trigger. The Greener jerked in his hands and recoiled. The dimmer light inside the warehouse was briefly illuminated by the powder flash as the shotgun boomed out its hard sound. The lethal twelve-gauge burst cut into the shooter as he attempted to take his follow-up shot. He fell back with a startled scream, clutching his bloody chest. Bodie had already moved, shotgun muzzle sweeping back and forth as he went deeper into the building. He picked up the steady crash of shots and imagined Brand delivering them as he routed the warehouse crew.

The scuff of boots on the hard timber floor warned Bodie of a close threat, and he ducked close to a row of packing cases, three high, using the shotgun to search around him. A handgun fired close by. The slug scored a burn across Bodie's left shoulder, a second missed by a fraction, and Bodie dropped, turning his upper body. His shotgun followed his actions, catching the dark-clad figure moving in, pistol following through. Bodie dropped the trigger, and the shotgun slammed out its heavy sound. The target's forward rush was brought to an abrupt stop as the Greener's full burst ripped into his body. As he fell, Bodie caught a glimpse of his bruised and battered face. It was Bennett, the big man who had braced him at the Barbary Coast saloon.

'That's what happens when you play sneaky,' Bodie said.

He broke the shotgun and plucked out the empty casings, then tossed them aside and reached into his pocket for fresh shot. His attention was drawn away from his surroundings for the scant seconds it took to reload. Out of the corner of his eye, he picked up a moving shadow to one side and higher up. He turned and saw a figure lunging down at him from the stacked packing cases.

The falling body slammed into him, the impact knocking him off balance. He slammed to the floor, losing his grip on the Greener. A black-clad Chinese man was standing feet away with a short-handled hatchet in his hand, the keen blade catching the light as he worked it back and forth. 'Fortune smiles on me,' he said in heavily accented English. 'First Henry Lee. Then Li Hung. And now the Gweilo who they called friend. Time for you to die, Bodie.'

# 21

This had to be Lo Keye, Tung's enforcer. The one who had caused the deaths of Lee and Hung.

Bodie pushed up off the warehouse floor, his right hand dropping to his side and sliding the Colt free. He raised the pistol, then felt a solid blow to his hand and felt the weapon jarred from his grip. The .45 was tossed aside. It hit the floor yards away. It was only then that Bodie saw Keye's right leg draw back from the kick he had launched, so fast he hadn't seen it coming. He pulled back, rising to his full height, and saw the hatchet in Keye's hand cutting the air. The weapon seemed to be part of his limb, his gestures smooth and fast. There was a thin smirk on Keye's lips as he demonstrated his skill.

*The hell with you, feller*, Bodie thought. *We can all bring a blade to the party*.

He dropped his hand to his side and grasped the knife sheathed on his belt. The razor-sharp weapon was the one he had taken from the half-breed Silverbuck and made his own. He'd had to kill the breed twice to make sure he finally stayed down, but Bodie only blamed himself for that. He should have made certain the first time round. His mistake had almost cost him his own life on their second meeting. It had taught the manhunter a lesson and left him with some serious injuries before he'd nearly cut off Silverbuck's damn head. As he brought the knife into view, Bodie warned himself not to make the same mistake again.

Keye registered the knife. His eyes flickered and he eased back a little. He was not showing fear — simply respect for the cold steel. The Tong enforcer was facing an opponent with his own weapon, not a defenseless individual with little chance to fight back. It made a difference. But Keye was far from being a novice himself.

Bodie watched the Chinese man, seeking the signs that Keye was about to go on the offensive and knowing he was going to need his wits about him. Keye was not going to make it easy . . .

Bodie saw Keye's forward right foot edge forward, his leg tense as he set himself, and leaned forward a little. He had turned the hatchet edge on to Bodie, ready to make a sweep that would cut across his torso. Though Bodie anticipated the move, it came almost too fast for him to counter. Keye's arm was a blur, the cold steel of the blade arcing round and shearing through Bodie's shirt as he pulled back. The cut, not as deep as intended, left a stinging wound that bled immediately. Bodie's response was to hit out with his own knife, catching Keye's right side as the man's body turned. The heavy blade slashed Keye's tunic and bit into his flesh over his ribs. The speed of Bodie's response had caught the Chinese off guard. He fell back, conscious of the blood streaming down his side from the gash.

Seeing a possible opening, Bodie lunged forward, his blade spearing in at Keye's torso. The strength behind the manhunter's move slammed him against Keye and they stumbled back, crashing against the stacked crates. Bodie felt his blade slide into Keye's left shoulder, grating against bone. The Chinese uttered a yell of pain and swung his hatchet at Bodie, but the closeness of their bodies stopped him making a clean strike. Bodie clamped his free hand around Keye's wrist and forced the hatchet clear of his body. Keye brought up his right leg, driving his knee into Bodie's side, a solid blow that hammered Bodie's ribs. In response, Bodie, still gripping the handle of his knife, concentrated his strength and pushed the blade deeper into Keye's shoulder, driving it all the way into the joint and out the other side, the exposed blade piercing the wooden crate the Chinese was pushed up against. In a moment of pure frenzy, Keye clamped his free hand across Bodie's face, fingers clawing at his cheeks. With the knife blade buried in his shoulder, Keye's hand had weakened and Bodie was able to wrench his head to one side, freeing himself from the hand over his face.

Keye's knee delivered a second blow to Bodie's ribs as the manhunter used both hands to put pressure on Keye's hatchet wrist, twisting it hard. Bodie felt the bone move, kept turning it until something snapped. Keye gave a yelp. Bodie maintained his grip, bending the wrist. Keye's fingers loosened their grip and the hatchet slipped free. Bodie made a grab for it, closed his fingers over the short handle. He struck out with the blade, the steel catching Keye across the side of his head, severing a bloody wedge of scalp. Keye, pinned to the crate, was unable to move aside. As blood streamed over his face, Keye was barely able to see the hatchet rise and fall before the blade bit into his skull. As Keye's body went into a spasm, Bodie reached and jerked his knife free, letting the bloodied body slide to the floor.

Tung and Traeger were standing beside a large wooden crate that had a lit oil lamp throwing illumination over the paperwork they had been discussing. Alerted by the shooting, they were on the defensive. A figure moved into view, confronting them.

'Nowhere left to run, Traeger. Your partnership with Tung ends here,' Brand said, drawing their attention. Brand had his Colt steady in his hand. He had holstered the adapted pistol, deciding the longer reach of his regular weapon would be more suitable at the moment.

'You realize the amount of money involved here, Brand?' Traeger said. 'When this deal is concluded, we'll be rich. You could have some of it. More than you could ever hope to see in your lifetime. I'm sure that must interest you.'

'Only to be able to return it to the people you stole it from. And then hand you over to stand trial for murder. So no deal, Traeger.'

Milo Traeger stood beside Kwai Fu Tung. The Tong Master was dressed in a gray suit, his shirt gleaming white against his skin. Where Traeger exhibited a nervous manner, Tung appeared calm, almost serene. His hands were lightly crossed at his waist.

'You've proved to be a competent man, Mr. Brand. As has your companion, Bodie. Rescuing the young woman from my people was enterprising. Two singularly expert people. A pity you work on the opposite side of the law. You've spumed Mr. Traeger's offer of money. Is there no way I could persuade you to step across the line and join my organization? Look around at what I have stored here. My organization is expanding even as we speak.'

'Even if I was tempted, Tung, there wouldn't be much incentive. No point in joining an outfit about to be closed down in the next few minutes.'

'I can guarantee that.' Bodie stepped

into view, his own pistol leveled at Tung. 'Game over, Tung. Your man, Keye, is back there. Kind of let that hatchet he used go to his head. So you won't be walking away this time.'

The Tong Master nodded slowly, the expression on his face never changing. 'Then we have no more to say.' Disregarding the pistol trained on him, he dipped his hand inside his coat, snatching at the slim-bladed knife sheathed in his belt. His move was a blur, hand going back then forward as he launched the weapon in Bodie's direction. Bodie had to give him credit for the speed of his action, leaning to one side as the knife flashed in his direction. It missed by a fraction, burying itself in one of the wooden crates nearby.

Tung had turned, preparing to conceal himself behind stacked goods. The Colt in Bodie's hand followed his move. He put three fast shots into the comer of the bales that briefly covered Tung. They emerged in a dusty cloud of opium and fragments of the cloth wrapped around the narcotic, and struck Tung in the body. He was toppled sideways, stumbling to his knees as the slugs hammered home. Bodie stepped up and raised his pistol again. He fired a final shot that slammed into Tung's skull and sent him face down.

'For Henry Lee and Li Hung, feller,' he said quietly.

Traeger stared open-mouthed at the body, watching the blood soaking through Tung's clothes. He drew his gaze away, easing his hands from his body in apparent surrender. 'I quit,' he said as Brand appeared, stepping from the shadows a few yards away.

'Damn right you do,' Brand said. 'Unless you want to end up like your partner.'

'Never would have lasted,' Traeger said. 'I don't think he liked me all that much.'

'Can't fault him there.' Brand gestured with his Colt. 'Time we got out of here.'

'No argument from me,' Bodie said.

Traeger stepped forward, showing little resistance. As he moved by the packing case where he had been standing with Tung, going over the loading manifests, he let his left hand reach out. He caught hold of the oil lamp being used for illumination, swept it clear of the case and slammed it to the floor. The lamp glass shattered, and spilled oil ignited with a soft whoosh of sound. Traeger kicked out at the lamp, the split base shedding more oil that created a burning pool. The glare of flame created a temporary barrier between Traeger and his captors as it licked at the dry wood of the warehouse floor and the stacked packing crates. Smoke started to rise. Traeger turned and headed towards the rear of the warehouse.

'Sonofabitch,' Bodie said.

'Well he's my sonofabitch,' Brand said. 'Take the outside in case he makes a break that way.'

Brand cleared the rising spread of burning oil as it ate at the dry cracked floor and headed in the direction Traeger had taken.

*No chance you're getting away now,* Brand promised.

# 22

It was definitely not the way he had expected things to end. Milo Traeger realized the whole scheme had fallen apart at the seams, and right now all that mattered was getting away. He didn't let the setback bring him down any further than accepting the facts. It was not the first time he had faced disaster, and as before, he had reached the point where his survival instinct took over. No looking back. No regrets. Simply forgetting everything except staying alive. Milo Traeger would melt into the woodwork, salvage what he could if possible, and move on. There would be other opportunities, and he would choose one and start again.

He sped through the cluttered warehouse, his destination the door at the rear of the building. He had located this the first time Tung had shown him around and kept it in mind. He had not mentioned it to Tung, not wanting to plant any suspicion that he might be ready to walk away. Keeping Tung sweet had been the order of the day then. But with Tung dead and the business deal unraveling, Traeger knew it was time for him to retreat.

He reached beneath his coat for the pistol he carried in a holster fastened to his belt, held close to his spine. He jerked the weapon free and held it in his hand as he kept moving. Traeger had no illusions. He was no skilled gunman. On the other hand, he would have no compunctions about pulling the trigger if it came to saving his life. Money aside, he held that notion dear. If he died, nothing else would matter, and he wanted to live for many more years.

As he slunk around the end of a line of bales, his feet went from under him and he dropped to his knees. He fell hard, yet managed to keep a grip on the pistol. His left hand, thrown out to steady himself, scraped across the rough wood. He felt a sudden pain, and almost immediately blood welled up from the torn skin.

'Damn.' Traeger scrambled to his feet, aware that his pants had been torn at the knees. He wiped his bleeding palm across his rumpled coat, breathing hard. Now he could feel burning pain where his knees had scraped on the floor. *Easy, Milo. You can always replace the clothing.*

He made out the narrow door at the far end of the warehouse, which was partly open; he could see daylight. His way out. His escape. A smile edged his lips. He could make it.

Throwing a quick glance over his shoulder, Traeger saw the way the flames had risen and spread. If they kept up, the whole warehouse could burn to the ground, taking everything with it. He thought briefly about the consignment of opium Tung had stored in the place, as well as the other contraband. All that hoard. What a waste. But the regret was fleeting. The loss didn't really matter;

not now. Other things had become more important to him.

He stumbled again in his rush, falling against stacked bales. The uppermost bundles slipped and thumped to the floor. Traeger righted himself, pausing for a few seconds. Something made him glance behind him.

And there was Brand, a pistol in his hand, moving in his direction with a determined step. Damn the man. Traeger triggered his own weapon in haste, wasting a slug. He saw it blow splinters from a crate. Yet Brand kept coming with no hesitation. The expression on his face was set, giving it a mask-like appearance.

Traeger lifted his pistol again, this time taking a moment to aim. His finger felt stiff against the trigger, and his hand trembled slightly. His shot this time was closer to the mark. It clipped Brand's left arm, jerking it aside. He was sure he saw fragments of cloth torn free, felt a surge of excitement, and set himself to fire again.

The shot was hard on his ears, but not from his gun. The lance of flame came from Brand's Colt with a puff of smoke. Traeger felt the hard impact as the .45 caliber slug hit him in the chest. He took a step back, his gun arm dropping to his side. The shot he was about to take exploded into the floor at his feet. The strike to his chest had placed the lead slug deep, shattering bone and tearing at his insides. He didn't hear the next two shots, but felt them as they ripped into him.

Now the pain made itself known. It flowered, and Traeger was suddenly down on his knees. The brassy taste of blood was in his mouth; there was no time to think about anything. The warehouse began to grow dim in his eyes as he slumped against the close stack of crates.

He only felt a tremendous stunning blow when Brand put his fourth slug into his skull. Then Milo Traeger's world shut down, and he sank into absolute darkness and utter silence.

# 23

By the time Inspector Hallows showed up at the warehouse, it had been reduced to a charred ruin. Smoke hung over the area, drifting as the breeze from the bay moved it. A crowd had gathered, curiosity attracting them, as such events always did. A horse-drawn fire engine finally arrived, but by then there was nothing to save. With the Tung warehouse having been isolated from any other structures, there had been no danger to other buildings.

Bodie and Brand had maintained a watch in case any of Tung's Tong soldiers put in an appearance, but none did. Smoke-streaked and bloodied, they stood at the edge of the dock, too weary to do anything else.

In the buggy that delivered Inspector Hallows was Sergeant Kilpatrick, accompanied by Dr. Boyd and Richard Hunt.

'You pair leave nothing standing in your wake,' the Irishman said.

Boyd looked quietly at the harm Bodie and Brand had suffered, making soft mutterings as he did what he could on the spot, making it clear he wanted both of them to return to his office as soon as possible.

'I take it there are bodies in there?' Hallows observed.

'Tung,' Brand answered. 'Traeger. A number of the ones working for them.'

'Tung's enforcer is one of them,' Bodie said. 'He told me he'd killed Harry Lee and the old Chinese feller, Li Hung.'

'They do say confession is good for the soul,' Hunt said.

'Yeah? Well his only got him a hatchet in the head.'

'I'll need written statements covering everything that happened,' Hallows said. 'I hope they justify my letting you pair take this as far as you have.'

'You'll get them,' Brand said. 'You'll be covered for all this, Inspector. My department will see to that. I can't speak for Bodie, but all I need right now is a chance to clean up and change into fresh clothes.'

'How's Jasmine?' Bodie asked.

'That young lady is doing fine, and looking forward to meeting her father as soon as he arrives in town,' Boyd informed him.

'That should be an interesting reunion,' Hunt said.

He was right as it was.

★   ★   ★

Mid-morning two days later, Brand and Bodie were at the station when the train arrived. Along with Chin Yi Soong was Lawyer Bainbridge and a surprise for Bodie in the form of Ruby Keoh. The moment she stepped down to the platform, she made for Bodie, hugging him with open affection.

'Are you badly hurt?'

'No more than usual.'

'You always make light of your condition,' she admonished him. Then

220

she added, 'And yes, I know it comes with the job.'

'It's getting unsettling,' Bodie said, 'the way you know me so well.'

Ruby's smile only exacerbated his concern. 'And this is Mr. Brand?'

'Miss Keoh. I've been looking forward to meeting you.'

'And I you.'

Chin Yi Soong had greeted his daughter and held her close as he met Bodie. 'Ruby's faith in you has been proved, Mr. Bodie. Words can't express my gratitude for what you've done. I'm in your debt.'

'No need. Seeing Jasmine back with you makes it worthwhile.'

'Sir, you've saved my daughter and my company. That man Traeger and his partner Tung would have ruined me and spread their vile opium across the city. But my greatest concern was for my Jasmine. So thank you again.'

Lawyer Bainbridge, a solemn-faced lean figure with a professional demeanor, shook Bodie's hand. 'If ever you need anything, Mr. Bodie, I'm at your disposal. Never hesitate to contact me.'

Bodie had not failed to notice the way the lawyer gazed at Jasmine with more than just a professional eye; and the way the young woman returned his attention made him realize her own feelings. No need to ask what was going on there.

'Mr. Brand, it would be remiss of me not to add my thanks for your hand in this matter,' Soong said. 'This was a sorry affair all round, but you are to be congratulated for your part. You can be sure Mr. McCord has been appraised.'

'Just doing my job, sir.'

'More than that,' Jasmine said. 'A great deal more.'

'My sentiments as well,' Soong said. He reached into his coat pocket and withdrew a buff envelope, handing it to Brand. 'This came for you.'

Brand knew what the telegram contained almost before he opened it. A smile edged his lips as he read McCord's to-the-point message.

As they all made their way from the platform, Bodie edged alongside Brand. 'He a happy man?'

'That'll be the day. Looks like I'll be moving on. He has something for me to investigate.'

'That feller gets his money's worth.'

'Doesn't he. At least I get a few days to settle things here before I need to pick up on this. And more damn paperwork.'

They shook hands as they crossed the platform. Ruby was heading towards them, her gaze fixed on Bodie.

'Seems you're going to have you own hands full,' Brand observed.

Bodie smiled. 'You're not wrong there, amigo,' he said. 'You're not wrong.'

Brand picked up the satisfied tone in Bodie's words. No regrets there at all. It reminded him of Virginia and Adam. Maybe there would be a chance to see them before he took up his next assignment. He was determined to make it happen, McCord be damned. Yet he couldn't help but try to imagine what his new assignment held for him . . .

THE KILLING DAYS
CREOLE CURSE

*BODIE MEETS BRAND:*
TWO GUNS NORTH

*BALLARD & McCALL:*
TWO FROM TEXAS
GUNS OF THE BRASADA
COLORADO BLOOD HUNT
COLTER'S QUEST

We do hope that you have enjoyed reading this large print book.

Did you know that all of our titles are available for purchase?

We publish a wide range of high quality large print books including:
**Romances, Mysteries, Classics**
**General Fiction**
**Non Fiction and Westerns**

Special interest titles available in large print are:
**The Little Oxford Dictionary**
**Music Book, Song Book**
**Hymn Book, Service Book**

Also available from us courtesy of Oxford University Press:
**Young Readers' Dictionary**
**(large print edition)**
**Young Readers' Thesaurus**
**(large print edition)**

For further information or a free brochure, please contact us at:
**Ulverscroft Large Print Books Ltd.,**
**The Green, Bradgate Road, Anstey,**
**Leicester, LE7 7FU, England.**
**Tel:** (00 44) **0116 236 4325**
**Fax:** (00 44) **0116 234 0205**